Hello.

Me I is Pig. I is big and pink (sometimes a bit brown if I has been rolling in mud). My best friend **Duck** says I has stopped growing; that I has reached my maximum size. But I don't think this is true. I is sure when I eats a lot I gets a bit bigger and when I don't eat so much, I gets a little bit smaller.

Duck and I lives on **Mr and Mrs Sandal's Farm**. We used to live here with just **COW** and all the **Sheeps**. That was until our last adventure, where we was joined by a **Turkey** called **Ki-Ki**.

Since he's arrived, he has lived with me in my house. I never thought I would want to be sharing my house with anyone.

But **Ki-Ki** is big and fluffy and makes the best pillow ever, so I really isn't complaining. Oh, and he is very nice too – which of course is more important than the pillow thing. Well, sort of.

He says one day he will move out and get a house of his own, but I don't think he really means this. Even though he has never said it I knows the idea of sleeping alone in the dark scares him.

Since he arrived **Ki-Ki** has been doing his very best to join in with the silly games we loves playing. But I can tell that deep down he is not REALLY enjoying them as much as we does. When we plays **COW'S** favourite game, **where's woc?**, he spends more of his time finding things to make jewellery out of than he does finding **COW**. He made quite an amazing ring for one of his

WHERE'S WOC?

scaly toes out of an old
nut the other day. He
was super proud of it.

He can't play Name
That Fart with us
because he has an "over-sensitive beak".
This is a huge shame. Name That Fart is
my most favourite game in the whole wide
world. And we has just made it even better
— now it isn't about just doing farts what
sounds like animals. You can do farts what
sounds like anything: tractors, spaceships,
submarines. The other day I did my best
one yet. Luckily for **Ki-Ki**, he was too far
away to smell it, but he still heard it.

"OMG, Pig! That is just totally and

utterly gross-mongous!" he shouted across the yard, placing his wings over his ears and making a face like he was about to be sick.

"**Wrong answer!**" **Duck** shouted back. "**It's not gross-mongous, it's a combine harvester! Ha! Ha! Ha!**"

Me and **Duck** found this VERY funny. **Duck's** not only my best friend, he's also the best guesser of my fart noises ever. We loves playing games together. **Duck** used to have a big family to play with, but then one night **FOX** came and gobbled them all up. Nasty, nasty **FOX**!!!

Ki-Ki says he doesn't mind not playing with us. He says he is just happy to be here with such fantastic friends. Before he met us he had never had any.

To say a **"super-special thank you"** to me for being his friend and for letting him share my shed, he has made me this new diary. I is super impressed – it looks just as good as any of the **Farmer**-made ones I has used before. I loves keeping a diary. I is not sure what to call this one. **Ki-Ki** has suggested I call it:

The absolutely fantabulously wonderful

diary of Pig &

all his

incredibly lovely

friends

But I thinks that is a little bit too long. So
I has decided to call it...

Oddsiday

Hello.

As this is the first time I has been writing in a while, I is feeling I should tell you what has been happening — that way when I starts to tell you what is actually happening right now, you will be understanding it better.

First I needs to tell you about the **Sandals** and how hard they has been working. The **Sandals** really is the most amazing **Farmers** anyone could want to live with. They is Vegytarian — this means instead of growing animals to eat, they grows yummy veggies. Owners what don't want to eat you is the best kind you can have.

They started off just growing a few. But their veggies is so tasty that other **Farmers** started wanting them too, so they has had to grow more and more. They has even had to make their veggie patch bigger to make space to grow them all.

I wishes that they would extend it into

my Pig House. It would be so amazing to have a bedroom filled with delicious turnips and yummy carrots. But maybe not that amazing for very long. I don't think I could help but eat them all up, and I know that would make **Mr and Mrs Sandal** EXTREMELY cross.

Anyways, **Mr and Mrs Sandal** works very hard. Every day they works from when the sun comes up, until the sun goes down. **Duck** says they has got a bad case of "**work-o-holism**". I hopes it is not catching. I wouldn't want to be working so hard ALL day. In fact I doesn't want to be working at all – that would stop me having so much time to play.

Work-o-holism makes you do some odd
things too. The other day **Mr Sandal** was
sitting in his special chair, singing away to
his veggies, when all of a sudden he fell
asleep. One minute I was listening to him
going, "**La, de, da, de, deeeee...**" and the next I
was listening to him snoring. He dribbled all

down his nice rainbow-
coloured jumper too.
Poor **Mr Sandal**.

And **Mrs Sandal**
is no better.
Yesterday she gave
me a bowl of **Sheeps'**
pellets instead of
my normal Piggy
slops. **Sheeps'** food is

YUCK! It makes my tongue go all dry
and funny. I tried to tell her that she
had made a mistake, but she just did a
big yawn, patted me on the head and
walked off.

The second thing I needs to tell you is

sort of strange and I feels a bit silly even saying it. But I has to, because it's really bothering me: I thinks I is being watched. I has no idea by who or what. I has never seen anyone watching me — which is why I know it sounds really silly. I just has this really strong feeling they is, and it won't go away.

It all started the other day when me and **Duck** was over at his pond trying to work out whether, if I did a big enough fart, I could fire

6

myself from one side to the other. I was trying to see how many seconds I could fart for without stopping (I managed six on my first attempt — woo-hoo!) and **Duck** was doing something he called "**mathematical calculations**" — he really is so smart. We had just decided it might be possible — if I lost a bit of weight, but remained just as farty — when all of a sudden all the little hairs on my body stands up on end and I gets this feeling like someone is looking at me: really staring. It felt horrible.

When I looked around to see who it was, I couldn't see anyone. **COW** was in her shed eating some hay, the **Sheeps** was all in their field busy scratching themselves against their fence (they is very woolly at the moment and this makes them extremely itchy) and **Ki-Ki** was over by the **Old Barn** looking for things to make himself a new necklace from.

I told **Duck** about my strange feeling, but he just laughed and said, "Who would want to spy on you? The fart police?" He found his joke really funny. I loves him very much, but he can be so annoying sometimes.

I guesses he is probably right though. Who would want to spy on me? I really isn't that interesting.

Badfartsyday

Hello.

Today we is all getting a big surprise. It pulled into the yard just after breakfast. **Duck** tells me it is called a Camper Van; **Farmers** travels around in them when

they wants a break from living in their
house. The Camper Van is painted all over
with flowers, rainbows, sunshines and birds.
On the side is a large picture
of a black cat. I has to say I
is really not sure about cats,
not after the last one I met
tried to kill me – I really
hopes there is not a real cat
inside the van!

The owner of the Camper
Van is the craziest-looking
lady **Farmer** what I has
ever seen. She has long grey
hair what is piled up on top
of her head like a giant

bird's nest. She wears a little round pair of glasses, what makes her eyes look bigger than they is, and in her ears she wears these enormous gold hoops. Her clothes is as bright and patterned as her van and she is wearing at least one hundred necklaces and bracelets. On her feet she wears the most AMAZING sandals. They makes the ones **Mr and Mrs Sandal** wear look VERY boring. They is covered all over in coloured beads and little, dangly, silver circles what makes a jingle-jangle sounds when she walks.

I can immediately tell that **Ki-Ki** likes her. **"Wow-wee! What a fantabulously**

beautiful creature," he says, fluffing out all his tail feathers, trying to get her attention.

Mrs Sandal runs over and gives the crazy-looking lady **Farmer** a huge hug. She says something to her, what **Duck** translates as meaning that she is **Mrs Sandal's** aunt. **Duck** listens in – he says she has come to look after us whilst **Mr and Mrs Sandal** go on something called a "Yoga Retreat". **Duck** says this is the perfect kind of holiday for **Farmers** like the **Sandals**. He tells me it involves spending every day eating veggies and bending into funny positions. This sounds like a very odd sort of holiday to me — I gets the eating part, but not the bending bit. How silly.

"So long as Mrs Jingle-Jangle feeds me delicious slops, I is sure I won't miss the **Sandals** too much," I says. **Ki-Ki** thinks my name for her is very funny. I is very good at making up names.

The **Sandals** shows Mrs Jingle-Jangle around the yard. She leaves her van open. So whilst they is busy looking at the veggie patch, me, **Duck** and **Ki-Ki** has a sneaky peek. It's just as amazing-looking on the inside. Everything is covered in patterns: her chair, her bed, her kitchen. And the ceiling

is completely covered in material what

makes it look like a starry sky.

Ki-Ki can't stop saying "OMG!"

I looks all around; I can see lots of

pictures of a cat, but luckily I can't see a real one – phew!

Just after lunch a big bus pulls up outside the gate. It has a large sunshine painted on the side, with a picture of a Farmer sitting in a very strange position in the middle of it. Inside it is full of other **Farmers** what looks just like Mr and Mrs Sandal. It beeps its horn and Mr and Mrs Sandal comes out of their house with some big bags. They gets on the bus and waves goodbye to us. Mrs Jingle-Jangle waves back. She jingles and jangles from top to bottom.

As we watches the bus drive away I gets my strange being-spied-on feeling again.

"**Duck**," I says, "I is being watched, just like I was the other day. I can feel it, I really can. Right now!"

"**Of course you're being watched**," says **Duck**, "**by all the Farmers on the bus. They have probably never seen such a big, pink Pig.**" He gives my tummy a little prod with his wing and laughs.

I spends the rest of the day trying to forget about it. Luckily Mrs Jingle Jangle

brings me my supper a bit early; slops
always takes my mind off things. I is
super excited to see what kind she
makes – every **Farmer's** is
different. I eats them up very
quickly, making lots of happy
oinking sounds. I really wants to impress
her with my eating skills. I can eat LOTS
very fast. She laughs and talks to me in
Farmer.

Duck translates for me: "**What a greedy
Piggy. You're just like a Hoover, gobbling up
anything and everything!**" Mrs Jingle-Jangle is
very funny. She thinks I is a Pig-Hoover –
a Poover. Ha! Ha! Ha!

I has to say though, if I is honest, I is not

enjoying Mrs Jingle Jangle's slops as much as I would like. They is very different to any I has had before – and not in good way. They tastes a bit like the way Mrs Jingle Jangle smells – of flowers. And they does terrible things to my bottom. After I has finished eating I does the strangest-smelling fart ever. It smells just like the roses what grows in the **Sandals**' garden. I is really not happy about this. Pig farts is NOT meant to smell nice.

My flowery farting makes **Ki-Ki** very happy though. They doesn't make him pass out, in fact just the opposite. He says he finds them **"totes delightful"** and praises Mrs Jingle Jangle for her genius new slops recipe. He even suggests a new fart game, **"Air Freshener or Flower?"** Where you has to guess which one my fart smells more like.

I is really not sure how I feels about any of this!

Spooksiday

Hello.

I has to say I has never seen **Ki-Ki** as happy as I has seen him with Mrs Jingle Jangle. It is not that he has been unhappy with us, it's just he seems to have found a whole new happiness with her.

I immediately likes her too. She may not make the best slops, but there is something gentle and kind about her. She gives us all nice pets and strokes. She also sings all the time. I likes the sound of her songs — they makes me feel happy.

I can tell, though, straight away, that **Ki-Ki** is her favourite. I is not jealous about this at all; in fact I is quite pleased. His last owner was so evil to him — he deserves someone nice to love him.

After Mrs Jingle Jangle has fed us all breakfast, and given us our pats and back scratches, she opens the door to her van and encourages **Ki-Ki** inside. He happily goes in and doesn't come out again for ages. As soon as he does I calls him over to **Duck's Pond** so he can tell us all about his visit. I has never been invited to spend time with a **Farmer**. I wonders what they gets up to inside their homes. Does they have sleeps like us? Does they play games?

Ki-Ki is so excited to tell us what happened that we doesn't even have to ask him.

"**Oh, it was soooo fantabulous,**" he babbles. "**She is in-credible. So nice and kind and caring. You know that cat she has pictures of everywhere? Well that used to be her cat. I think its name was Moonstone. Only something terrible happened to it. I noticed she had a picture of this little cat-shaped gravestone. It had** Farmer **writing on. I could just understand the words 'Cruelly eaten' and 'Neighbour's dog'. How tragic!**"

He lets out a very brief, sad sigh.

"Anyway, get this, I think she wants me to be her new Moonstone. I think it's 'cos I'm just like him. I have the same colour tail as he did: black with white bits at the end — spooky, right?! When Mrs Jingle Jangle noticed it, she started stroking it, saying Moonstone's name over and over.
In that moment I think we both really connected, you know, like, spiritually."

Duck does a little swirly sign with his wing next to his head, **"Crazy!"** he mouths at me.

"So you didn't play any games at all?"
I asks, slightly disappointed. I hoped I was
going to learn about some new ones.

"**Well**," says **Ki-Ki**, excitedly flapping
his wings, "**we did do some Tea Leaf
Reading. That's kind of
like a game. You take a
cup of tea, and when it's
almost finished you
look inside and
study the leftover
tea leaves. You
look at these
and they tell you
what's going to happen to you.** Mrs Jingle
Jangle **did a reading for me. She said I**

was 'destined for high places'. How exciting is that?! Me, Ki-Ki, becoming something marvellicious. Now I know how it works I could read your fortune for you if you like?"

"But I doesn't drink tea," I points out.

"No problemo," says Ki-Ki, "I am sure slops will work just the same. Come on, let's give it a go."

I is pretty sure it's a waste of time. If my slops is telling Ki-Ki anything, it'll be that I'm going to do some more flowery farts. But he is so excited about doing it that I feels I has to let him.

So when Mrs Jingle Jangle brings me my supper slops I leaves a bit of them in the bottom of my bowl. I has to say, for once, this is not hard to do; today they tastes even weirder.

Duck and me watches **Ki-Ki** as he swirls them round and round. He asks if I can do one of my nice new farts, to help create **"the perfect ambience"**. I manages to conjure one up. It smells like the yellow flowers what come out in springtime.

"Air freshener," says **Ki-Ki**, sniffing. **"No. Hang on. Sorry, wrong: flower. Primrose, yes, definitely primrose. Am I right? Am I right?"**

He looks over at me as he swirls. I rolls my eyes and shakes my head. I is NOT playing this game!

"**Spoilsport!**" he says.

Finally he stops swirling. Me and **Duck** gives each other a "this should be funny" look. **Ki-Ki** peers into the gooey mess in the bottom of my bowl and jumps back in horror.

"**No!**" he cries, covering his beak with his wings. "**Oh no!**"

"Oh no, what?" I asks. "Is my farts about to go back to the great-smelling ones you hate?"

"**It's much worse that that,**" he says, not finding me funny. "**Something terrible** is going to happen to you. Something really terrible!"

"His farts is going to smell like primroses FOR EVER," laughs **Duck**.

"**No**," says **Ki-Ki**, getting very cross. "**It's serious — really serious!**"

"**Primroses. That would be serious, right, Pig?**" says **Duck**, giving me a nudge. I laughs along with him, then I remembers all the funny feelings I has been having about being watched — what if **Ki-Ki's** fortune telling has something to do with this?

I continues to laugh with **Duck**, but inside I is not thinking it is all quite as funny as it was a minute ago.

Terrornight

Hello.

It's the middle of the night and I is lying in my bed wide awake — I can't sleep. In fact, I is not sure I is going to be able to sleep ever again, not after what I thinks I has just seen!

Like normal I falls asleep on **Ki-Ki** dreaming about eating yummy veggies — ones what doesn't taste like flowers! I has just dream-eaten my way through 12 carrots, 37 potatoes and 9 turnips, when I feels a strange pressure on my tummy. I thinks it must just be a dream-fart forming, but the pressure doesn't move towards my bottom, it moves up towards my head. Up it creeps, closer and closer, until suddenly I feels a stab of pain just above my eye. Farts never come out of your eyes. Not even dream ones!

I opens one eye and looks around to see if I can see what hurt me. At first everything is black and blurry, but as my eye begins to see in the dark I starts to make out a dark shape staring down at me.

Something is standing on top of my head.

A terrible, scary something.

One what I never

thought I would ever see again.

My heart freezes. I is sure it really does. I can't feel it beat.

Panic fills up my whole body. Even though I wants to get up and run away I can't.

I lets out a tiny frightened gasp.

"**YOU!**" it whispers in a silly, posh-sounding accent, moving its horrible face even closer to mine. "**YOU ARE A VERY DEAD PIG!**"

It throws its head back and softly lets out a horrible laugh.

Surely I can't be seeing what I is seeing...

THE SUPER EVIL CHICKEN IS BACK!!!!

KLA! KLA! KLA!

I lets out a small frightened fart. The **SUPER EVIL CHICKEN** sniffs and lets out another nasty, silent laugh. I is not surprised it finds it funny — my fart smells like the blue plant **Mrs Sandal** grows in a pot by her front door.

"**Mmmmmm, lavender**," says **Ki-Ki** dreamily. I don't think the **SUPER EVIL CHICKEN** realized he was there. He stares down at him in surprise. I glances down too and when I looks back up the **SUPER EVIL CHICKEN** is gone. Vanished! Like it was never there. I looks all around my shed, and then all around it again. No sign.

My heart springs back to life.

Ki-Ki turns over.

"Are you awake?" I whispers, hoping he is
so I can tell him what just happened and
how frightened I is.

"**Yes**," he mutters back and lets
out a little snore, "**I am your new
Mooooonstone.**" He's sleep talking.

I lays my head back down and closes
my eyes. But I can't get back to sleep.
I can't get the picture of the **SUPER**

EVIL CHICKEN out of my head.

Surely – I tries to convince myself – surely it was just a nightmare? After all, a real **EVIL CHICKEN** couldn't just disappear, right?

Worryday

Hello.

I is so tired. I hasn't slept one wink. I is very glad it is morning though, so I can tell someone about what happened.

Ki-Ki had no idea who the **EVIL CHICKENS** was, so me and **Duck** filled him in. We told him how horrible they were. How they used to live in a shed next to mine, how I used to fart into it to pay them back for being so nasty. We told him how, one day, they tricked me into flying to Pluto in the Trocket they had built, and how when I finally got back, **Duck** and me got our revenge by rocketing their shed into space, with them and my old **Farmer** (who wanted to chip-chop me up and eat me) inside.

"**And you think these hideous CHICKENS are back?**" he asks when we has finished. "**That they came into your shed last night whilst we were sleeping?**"

"Well, yes, sort of," I says.

"**OMG! I so told you!**" he says, fanning his face with his wings, getting all over-excited. "**Your slops said something totally terrible was going to happen — they must have meant this!!!!!**"

"Honestly, you two!" says **Duck**. "You're as crazy as each other. We sent the **EVIL CHICKENS** into space – we saw them go.

There was no steering wheel in their shed. There is no way they could have turned it around and come back down to Earth. What is a lot more possible is that Mrs Jingle Jangle's funny new slops gave you some strange dreams."

"But it didn't feel like a dream," I protests, "it felt VERY real."

"We all have dreams that feel real sometimes. I had one the other day where I grew huge wings, as big as an eagle's, and instead of my head I had COW'S. I tried to fly, but my COW

head was just too heavy. I was flapping my wings as fast as I could, but I just couldn't leave the ground. I woke up actually flapping my wings. It all felt so real. But of course it wasn't; it was just a silly dream," says Duck.

Wow! How can he call me and **Ki-Ki** crazy when he has dreams like that?!

"**Come on,**" he says, "**let's go and find COW and see if she wants a game of where's woc?** – that'll keep your mind off all this silly nonsense."

I can tell **Ki-Ki** is just as worried as I is. He even comes and plays **where's woc?** with us just so he can keep an eye on me.

I tries my hardest to enjoy it, but wherever I looks my silly brain makes me

see the **SUPER EVIL CHICKEN**. I looks under
the big flowerpot, there it is smiling back
at me. I lifts up the wheelbarrow, there
it is waving. It's even there when I peers
into the big tank what *Mr and Mrs Sandal*
collects rain in to water
their veggies with. Its
evil reflection stares
back at me and winks.

I gets so freaked out
by this that I makes
an excuse about
feeling overtired and
goes back to my shed for a lie down. I hear
Ki-Ki and **Duck** carry on the search for
COW without me. Finally they finds her

hiding behind the pointy arrow thing on top of the barn, what tells you which way the wind is blowing.

I closes my eyes and tries to sleep, but even though I is super tired, I just can't. The **SUPER EVIL CHICKEN**'s face is always there, staring straight back at me. It's

like its face is painted on the inside of my eyelids. It's horrible.

I REALLY, REALLY, REALLY wants **Duck** to be right about us both being silly. Normally I would want him to be wrong, but not this time.

Trauma-Morn

Hello.

Duck was right. I was wrong to think the **EVIL CHICKENS** was back and about to do something bad. They hasn't done anything terrible.

I HAS!

I've done something far, far worse and more evil than they ever could. I is now the evil one. I IS EVIL PIG!

I was so tired from not sleeping the night before that, by the time I went to bed, I was totally exhausted. **Ki-Ki** made himself into the biggest, softest pillow, which made sleeping even easier.

Just before sunrise I starts to have this dream about the biggest turnip ever. It's a super, ginormous whopper. When I bites into it, it's more juicy than any turnip I has ever tasted — all nice and mushy. My dream tummy is super happy. Yum! Yum! Yum! I is just about to take the final bite when I gets this funny feeling in my mouth. It feels like it is full of something dry and tickly, like feathers. It's horrible. I starts to cough so much that I wakes myself up.

I feels my straw bedding pressing against my cheek. That's funny, I thinks, as I lets out another splutter, where's my **Ki-Ki** pillow gone? I lifts my head up to look for him and chokes again. Feathers, real ones not dream ones, puffs out of my mouth. I looks down at them; they is the same colour as **Ki-Ki's**. Why is I spitting out his feathers?

I calls out his name, but I gets no reply. He's not here. I calls out louder, but still nothing. Mrs Jingle Jangle's voice suddenly pops into my head: "You're like a Hoover," it says.

"You'd gobble up anything and everything!"

A terrible thought crosses my mind. It sends a cold tingle all the way down my back. What if I have, by mistake, in my sleep, eaten **Ki-Ki**? What if I can't see him because he is INSIDE MY TUMMY?

NO! NO! Surely not. I can't have. That would be impossible. Pigs only eat veggies. I would NEVER eat another animal.

I must be mistaken. He must have got up super early and gone to see Mrs Jingle Jangle. I runs over to her van and I calls out his name. "**Ki-Ki! Ki-Ki!** Are you in there?"

Mrs Jingle Jangle opens the door and looks down at me. She's clearly only just woken up, her crazy hair looks even more crazy and she is still wearing her **Farmer** night clothes. She rubs her eyes and blinks. I sneezes; some more feathers puff out of my mouth. Mrs Jingle Jangle lets out a loud scream. I tries to push past her and peek inside her van. I can't see **Ki-Ki** in there.

"Get back! Get Back!" she cries, pushing me out of the door. She doesn't even bother putting on her jingly-jangly sandals; she runs straight across the yard, to my shed, in her bare feet. She looks all around it for **Ki-Ki** I tries to tell her, "He's not here!" But of course Mrs Jingle Jangle doesn't understand Pig.

"Moonstone! Moonstone!" she cries out as she runs around the yard.

"**Ki-Ki! Ki-Ki!**" I cries, running around like a mad Pig after her. All the shouting wakes up **Duck** who comes paddling across his pond to see what is going on.

Before he can even ask, Mrs Jingle Jangle stops calling for "Moonstone" and turns on me. Her kind face suddenly doesn't look so kind. It looks very angry and very upset. She points her finger at me and says something in **Farmer**. Her lovely soft voice doesn't sound soft any more.

"**What on Earth????**" says **Duck**, looking very confused. "**She says she thinks you've eaten Ki-Ki!**"

"I ... I..." I stutters. To begins with I is too scared to even say the words, but then they tumbles out all at once. "... I thinks she might be right. Last night I dreamt I was eating the biggest, juiciest turnip ever – it was so delicious – but when I woke up my mouth was full of feathers – **Ki-Ki's** feathers – and he wasn't in my house and he isn't in Mrs Jingle Jangle's van and he isn't in the yard and..." I coughs and another feather comes out. It lands at **Duck's** feet – it's one of **Ki-Ki's** tail feathers. "... I thinks I has, by mistake, gobbled him up in my sleep."

I can see **Duck** is having a job to take this all in. His beak opens but no words come out.

"pig licker???" shouts **COW** from her shed. I had no idea she was listening in too. **COW** has a habit of getting her words in

Pig all muddled up, I am sure
she doesn't mean licker.
She means KILLER.
A Pig-killer — a Piller.
For the first time I
has made up a name I doesn't find funny
at all.

Our shouting must have woken the **Sheeps**
too 'cos I hears them shouting from their
field:

I looks at **Duck** for some sort of translation. This is not a word I has ever heard. He tells me it means I loves to eat meat.

I feels sick, sick all the way from my nose to my tail. How could I have done such a thing? How could I eat a friend? How could I have turned into a Carnivaar? I doesn't know whether to cry or scream, so I does both. I makes this terrible wailing sound. I feels so confused and strange. I doesn't know what to do. I runs back into my house and throws myself on to the straw.

I screams and cries all at once, thumping my trotters into the ground. Mrs Jingle Jangle

rushes over, slams my door and locks it. I
doesn't blame her. I would lock me up too. I
looks up at her; tears is running down my
face, snot is pouring out of my nose and I
thinks I is drooling too. Mrs Jingle Jangle looks
terrified.

Duck comes in and tries to calm me down.

"Get out!" I shouts. "I can't be trusted! I might eat you too! Get out! Get out!" The last thing I wants to do is, by mistake, eat my best friend.

"I know you, Pig. You're not going to eat me," says **Duck** calmly. **"I don't believe you have eaten Ki-Ki, either. Something very strange is going on here and I'm determined to get to the bottom of it. This all smells very fishy to me."**

I sniffs the air. I can't smell fish. **Duck** is going mad, just like me.

I sits down and I sobs and I sobs and I sobs. I wants to lie down and sleep and pretend like it all never happened but I can't; all my tears and dribbling has made my bed too wet.

Shocker-Noon

Hello.

I feels terrible and I is sure I looks terrible too. I has spent most of the morning crying. My face feels all swollen and puffy.

Mrs Jingle Jangle doesn't bring me any lunch. Why would she? She thinks I just ate **Ki-Ki**. This doesn't bother me; I isn't hungry. I guesses **Ki-Ki** has really filled me up. Yuck! Yuck! Yuck! Just the thought of what I has done makes me start to shake. Once I starts I can't stop.

Mrs Jingle Jangle does come over and see me though. She brings a big book with her.

"**Uh-oh!**" I hears **Duck** say from outside my shed. "**The Scientific Encyclopedia of Animal Diseases.**"

I wonders if he has been sitting outside all along.

She takes a good look at my dribbling, snot-covered face and shaking body and starts flipping through the book. She stops on a page near the middle and reads it quietly to herself. I hears her mutter some odd-sounding **Farmer** words: "Mucous." "Dribbling." "Fever." When she is finished she looks even more frightened than she was earlier.

"AHHH!" she cries, "SWINEY FLUE!!"

She slams the book shut and runs back into her van.

"**Swine Flu!**" says **Duck**, popping his head into my shed. "**She thinks you have Swine Flu. Really? This is all getting very, very silly.**"

"How has I caught Swiney Flue?" I asks. "Is it like work-o-holism? Did I get it from the **Sandals**? Does it make you eat your friends?"

"**NO, it's nothing like what the Sandals have. NO, it doesn't make you eat your friends. And most importantly, NO, you don't have it,**" he says. "**You aren't ill; there is nothing wrong with you. YOU DIDN'T EAT KI-KI! Like I said before, something very strange is going on here. Ask yourself this: could you taste anything**

funny in your mouth this morning, apart from feathers? Cast your mind back – think."

I tries to remember. My mind is such a muddle — it's hard.

"I think I just tasted turnip," I says. "But I really can't be sure. Maybe turkeys taste a bit the same?"

"Turkeys DO NOT taste like turnips!" says **Duck**. I can tell he is starting to get cross. Though I is not sure it is with me; I think it's with the pickle I is in.

"I don't understand. How could I have not eaten him?" I asks. I so wants **Duck** to be right about all this, but I just can't see how.

"Because Pig, I think you've been set-u—"

But before he can finish his voice is drowned out by a loud siren. I peers out through the bars on my gate to see where it's coming from. Into the yard screeches a white van.

This van is smaller than Mrs Jingle Jangle's and it doesn't have pretty patterns painted down the sides. It has five **Farmer** letters: **DEFRA**. It has one small window,

but instead of curtains it has metal bars.
And on its roof it has a blue flashing light.

Its doors burst open and two
Farmers steps out. Well, I thinks
they is **Farmers**. They could also be
space aliens, but I don't
think space aliens drive
Farmer vans.

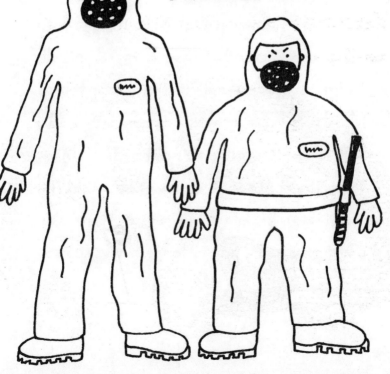

They is wearing large white suits what covers their whole bodies, white wellies, white gloves and these odd helmets on their heads what looks like buckets with special windows cut into them so they can see out.

Where their noses should be they has these big black circles, what makes a loud hissing noise when they breathe. All I can really see of their faces is their eyes. They doesn't look friendly. One is big and tall and one is much smaller and more round.

Mrs Jingle Jangle comes rushing out and points them towards my shed. The big one is carrying a strange head collar what has lots of looping straps dangling off it. The little one is carrying a long, black stick.

They walks over to my house and unbolts my door. When they talks, their special helmets makes them sound like they is hissing like snakes. They sounds just as evil as they looks.

They opens out their arms and walks towards me, forcing me into the corner of my house. The small one presses a button on the side of his stick. Little bolts of blue light flies out the end of it. It makes a nasty electric buzzing noise.

He points it at me.

"What's happening? What's happening?" I calls out in a panic. "Who are these odd **Farmers**?"

I can tell they must be super bad, 'cos **Duck** is attacking the big one's wellies, trying to stop him getting any closer.

"**DEFRA**," says **Duck**, dodging a kick.

"Deathra?" I says, finding it hard to hear him over their hissing.

"**You might as well call them that**," says **Duck**. "**This is bad, Pig!** Mrs Jingle Jangle **must have told them you have Swine Flu. They have come to take you away!**"

"TAKE ME AWAY! NO! NO!!!! THEY CAN'T, THEY CAN'T. THIS IS MY HOME," I screams. But then a big thought hits me: if I is a Carnivaar and I stays here, I might eat more of my friends. Wouldn't everyone be safer if I wasn't around?

Before I has time to think this thought through, Big Deathra lunges at me and throws his arm around my neck. He squeezes so hard I can't breathe. I feels my eyes bulge. With his other arm he takes the strappy head collar and roughly pulls it over my head.

He lets go of my neck, and tightens the straps around my head.

He attaches a lead to it and gives it a hard tug. It pulls me forwards. I loses my balance and falls over. He continues pulling. I tries to stand up but I loses my balance and falls over again. Little Deathra jabs at my head with the electric stick. I manages to move out of the way just in time. I hears it crackle and snap as it passes my ear. Big Deathra doesn't even wait for me to get up; he just drags me across the yard on my side.

"I won't let this happen to you!" says **Duck,** running along beside me. **"I won't, Pig, I promise! I will do everything to save you!"**

"Save me from what?" I wants to ask, but my mouth is clamped too tightly.

COW rushes out of her shed, snorting and looking very mad. Steam comes out of

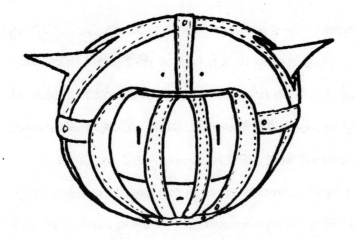

her nose — she pounds the ground with her
front hoof. Little Deathra lunges towards
her with the electric stick. She backs away.

I hears her cry as I is roughly bundled
into the back of the van. Just before the
doors slams shut I glimpses Mrs Jingle Jangle's
face. She looks upset and angry all at once.

The doors is slammed shut, the engine
roars and we speeds off. I manages to pick

myself up off the floor just in time to get my last glimpse of the **Farm** through the small back window. I sees Mrs Jingle Jangle, **COW**, the Sheeps and **Duck** all vanish into the distance.

I has a horrible feeling that will be the last time I will ever be seeing my friends. And, thanks to this stupid collar thing holding my mouth shut, I didn't even gets to say goodbye.

Unbelievable-Eve

Hello.

I don't think any slops would have been able to predict what has happened to me. Not even proper ones what doesn't taste like a field of flowers.

The van turns a sharp corner and I falls over. I can't be bothered to try and stand back up. It's going so fast I would just fall down again. As I lies there feeling very sorry and sad I lets out a little sigh.

"**SOLDIER!**" barks a gruff voice from behind me. "**GET A GRIP! REMEMBER: YOU CAN BE DESTROYED — BUT NEVER DEFEATED.**" I looks around trying to see who it came from.

I knows it's not Deathra; they can't speak Pig. In the gloom, in the far corner, I can just make out a small cage, and in the cage is a little **DOG**. I has never met a **DOG** before. I has seen them, from a distance, rounding up the **Sheeps** across the valley, but this one doesn't look like those **DOGS**. It's smaller, and it's white all over apart from two brown patches, one on its tummy and one over its eye.

I wants to say, "My name is Pig, not soldier," but it comes out as, "Mm nmmms iggg, nttt oljer."

"LOOKS LIKE YOU'RE IN TROUBLE, SOLDIER. WELL, YOU'RE IN LUCK. THIS OLD DOG'S BEEN WAITING FOR HIS NEXT MISSION. LOOKS LIKE

YOU'RE IT!" He takes off his collar and jiggles
the pin of its buckle into the lock on his
door. It clicks open.

"CLOSED SHACKLE PADLOCK. AN EASY PICK,"
he says calmly, like he does this kind of
thing every day.

As he walks over to where I is lying I
notices he only has three legs; one of his
back ones is missing. But this doesn't seem
to bother him. In fact he is way more
steady on his three feet than I is on my
four. The swaying van
doesn't affect him at
all. Using his collar pin he
undoes the padlock on my
muzzle.

If feels so nice to be able to move my mouth again. "Who are you?" I asks.

"THE NAME'S RUSTY. THAT'S ALL YA NEED TO KNOW FOR NOW."

I tries to introduce myself, but he just carries on talking over the top of me.

"NO TIME FOR PLEASANTRIES. TIME'S AGAINST US, SOLDIER. WE'LL LEAVE THE MEET 'N' GREET FOR LATER. RIGHT NOW DEATH'S IMMINENT. ESCAPE'S PRIORITY NUMBER ONE!"

"Death?" I asks, managing to squeeze a word in amongst all of his. "I thought I was just being taken to a place where I can't hurt anyone else."

"WE'RE NOT OFF TO A HOLIDAY CAMP, SOLDIER! THIS AIN'T NO FUN BUS! YOU AND I ARE BOOKED

70

ON A ONE-WAY RIDE. THEY'RE GONNA TAKE US OUTTA ACTION — PERMANENTLY." He draws a line across his neck. "SAYONARA, SOLDIER."

"Well, I'm a Carnivaar!" I says firmly. "I ate a friend. Maybe I deserves my punishment." As the words come out of my mouth I realizes I wants to take them back. I doesn't want my punishment to be death — what is I saying??? Maybe I really has got swine flu and gone mad.

"WE ALL HAVE TO LOSE OURSELVES IN ORDER TO FIND OURSELVES," barks RUSTY. "WHEN YOU REACH ROCK-BOTTOM THERE'S ONLY ONE PLACE LEFT TO GO. BACK UP. TODAY'S NOT A DAY TO DIE. TODAY'S A DAY TO BUST THIS JOINT. YOU WITH ME?"

I gives him a nervous little nod. I has no idea what he is saying or what "busting this joint" is. But it is all sounding better than what Deathra are about to do.

"I CAN'T HEAR YOU, SOLDIER! I SAID, 'ARE. YOU. WITH. ME?'" he barks, gruffly moving his face closer.

"Yes, RUSTY, yes!" I says, much louder, nodding as hard as I can.

"GOOD!" he says, giving me a wink. "THEN LET'S DO THIS THING. FOLLOW MY LEAD."

He takes a short run up and then starts hurling himself back and forth against the sides of the van, yelping and barking. For a small DOG he makes a lot of noise. I stands up and copies him. Where I slams into the side of the van, large Pig-shaped dents appear. Soon the back of the van is all bent out of shape. I has no idea why we is doing this, apart from to make a big mess, but it soon becomes clear. The van screeches to a stop and I hears Deathra get out and walk around to the back doors.

They throws them open and looks inside. **RUSTY** cowers in the back of the van, whimpering. I can tell from the looks on their faces they thinks I has been beating him up, or worse, trying to eat him up. They looks at the sides of the van, at the damage I has done, and lets out angry hisses.

Behind me I hears **RUSTY** quietly counting, "**THREE, TWO, ONE...**"

And before I knows it he is sprinting
down the van and throwing himself between
Big and Little Deathra.

he cries as Deathra ducks out of the way
to avoid him.

He lands on the road and sprints off
towards the woods what runs along both
sides of it.

"IT'S DO OR DIE, SOLDIER! C'MON. JUMP!" RUSTY
shouts back at me.

Big Deathra hisses something at the
Little one. He pulls the electric stick out
of the strap around his middle. He flicks it
on; even bigger sparks than before flies
out of the end. Before I even has a chance
to think what I is doing, I follows RUSTY'S
lead. I runs as fast as I can towards the
back doors. I is much bigger than him,
there is no way I is going to be able

to jump between Deathra. So instead, I smashes into them, knocking them both over backwards.

"ST-RIIIIIKE!!!!!" I hears **RUSTY** cheer.

I looks down at Deathra lying on the road, panting and groaning. I has totally winded them.

"THIS WAY, SOLDIER!" shouts RUSTY from the woods. I runs as fast as I can, following the sound of his voice. My four Pig legs has to work super hard to catch him up — he's really fast. Behind us I hears Deathra crashing through the woods, hissing and snarling.

RUSTY niftily dodges through the trees. Deeper and deeper we goes. I has never been into woods before. I has only looked out at the ones behind my shed; the ones what FOX lives in.

They is much darker inside than I imagined and much more tangly. Underneath the trees is lots of little brambles and bushes. RUSTY easily twists and turns to avoid them, but I is too big, all I can do is crash straight through. We runs and we runs for what feels like for ever. My lungs feels like they is on fire and my body stings from all the bramble cuts.

We keeps on going and going until, finally, I falls over, or I should say somersaults over. I is running so fast that I doesn't see the fallen tree trunk until it is too late. I hits it and flips right over the top of it. I lands flat on my back on the other side. I would celebrate the fact that I has just done my first-ever

somersault, but I is in too much pain.

"GOOD THINKING, SOLDIER PIG. REGROUP AND REASSESS," says RUSTY, rolling in underneath the fallen trunk next to me. He pricks up his ears and listens. I tries to listen too, but all I can hear is myself wheezing and groaning.

"Have ... we ... lost them?" I manages to croak.

"AFFIRMATIVE," says RUSTY. "WE'VE LOST OUR TAILS."

I checks, but my tail is still very much attached to my bottom and so is his. This must be more crazy soldier speak. I wishes **Duck** was here with me — he'd love all these odd phrases.

I is so pleased that we has escaped Deathra that for a moment I forgets all the bad stuff and lets out a little happy fart.

"**HOLY MOLY, SOLDIER!**" says **RUSTY**, sniffing the air. "**WHAT'VE YOU BEEN EATING? POTPOURRI?**"

"I, err, was fed some funny slops," I says, feeling myself blush all over. I really wishes my farts would just go back to normal.

"**NO KIDDING! THAT'S QUITE SOME FLOWERY FRAGRANCE YOU GOT GOING ON THERE,**" he laughs. "**NOW, SOLDIER, FARTS ASIDE, I WANT A DEBRIEF. I NEED TO KNOW WHAT I'M DEALING WITH HERE. YOU SAY YOU ATE A FRIEND. WHO D'YA CHOW DOWN ON? APART FROM THE ODD ROSEBUSH OR TWO? HA! HA! HA!**"

"I'm pretty sure I ate my friend **Ki-Ki**, a turkey," I says, hanging my head in shame.

"**DON'T BLAME YA, SOLDIER. TURKEY SURE IS A FINE-TASTING BIRD**," he says, licking his lips.

"But I doesn't want to be a Carnivaar. I doesn't want to eat other animals — especially not ones I really likes!" I protests.

"**LISTEN IN, SOLDIER PIG. I'VE GOT SOME NEWS FOR YOU. PIGS AIN'T CARNIVORES!**" he says, prodding me with his paw.

"Really? We're not?" I says, suddenly feeling some sort of hope.

"**NO, PIGS ARE OMNIVORES. MEANS YOU LIKE YOUR MEAT AS WELL AS YOUR VEG. YOU GREEDY BUNCH!**"

My heart sinks. I so hoped he was going to say we was Vegytarian, just like I thought.

If I is an Omnivore then of course I could have eaten **Ki-Ki Duck** was wrong. If only I had known this before, I would never have let **Ki-Ki** sleep in my shed with me. I didn't know I was so dangerous to be around.

It starts to rain. I huddles in underneath the trunk with **RUSTY**; I doesn't worry about by mistake eating him — he's so tough I reckons he could probably fight me off with just his tail.

"I SAY WE GET SOME ZEDS," he says, curling up. **"WE AIN'T GOIN' NOWHERE IN THIS DOWNPOUR."** He closes one eye and falls asleep, snoring softly. Amazingly the other eye stays open, constantly looking around — looking for danger.

I can't believe that yesterday I was happily living on the **Farm** with all my friends, and now here I is, in a dark wood, with a crazy three-legged **DOG**. I is glad that he saved me from horrible Deathra, but what is I going to do now? I can't live in the woods for ever. I has no idea how to live in the wild. What will I eat?

As the rain gets heavier and heavier, so does my heart.

Zero Six Hundred Hours

Hello.

I has decided that now I is being called Soldier that I should use soldier names for my diary days. I thinks this makes them sound much more exciting — not that they isn't of course. Anything you does as a soldier is exciting — well, sort of.

I is woken very early by a noisy mouse scrabbling around in a nearby bush. Woods is very noisy places, especially at night; everything rustles and squeaks.

The sun is only just starting to rise, but **RUSTY** is already up. He's hanging by his front paws from a nearby tree, pulling himself up and down.

"I LOVE THE SMELL OF SWEAT IN THE MORNING," he says, huffing and puffing. "ONE HUNDRED PULL-UPS EVERY DAY. IT'S WHAT KEEPS THIS SOLDIER FIGHTING FIT. YOU SHOULD TRY IT, SOLDIER PIG. SOON TURN THAT FAT PACK INTO A SIX PACK!"

I looks down at my big belly and blushes.

"Hey! Go easy there," I hears a familiar voice shout from above me. "I'm the only one who's allowed to tease him about his weight. Right, Pig?"

I looks up. Surely it can't be. It is...

"**DUCK!**" I cries with delight as he lands with a soft plop in front of me. I so wants to hug him, but then I remembers the Omnivore thing and backs away.

"**A COMRADE OF YOURS, SOLDIER PIG?**" says **RUSTY**, saluting **Duck**.

"**Yes**," says **Duck**, doing a little salute in return. "**I am Duck, Pig's best friend. I tracked him here. I couldn't let him be taken away**

without saying a proper goodbye." He waddles over to me and gives me a little nudge with his wing. **"Could I, my farty old friend?"**

"QUITE SOME TRACKING SKILLS YOU'VE GOT THERE, SOLDIER Duck," says **RUSTY,** looking impressed.

"Yes, I was worried I wouldn't be able to track the van on the road, but once I realized you'd run off into the woods it got a lot easier," says **Duck. "Old Pig here leaves quite a trail of destruction in his wake."**

"HMMMM, YES," says **RUSTY. "FIRST ON MY LIST OF POINTS TO ADDRESS. WE AIN'T GONNA EVADE CAPTURE FOR LONG WITH BIGFOOT HERE CREATING HIS OWN SUPER HIGHWAY WHEREVER WE GO! NOW, SOLDIER Duck, SOLDIER PIG TELLS**

ME HE'S EATEN SOMETHING HE SHOULDN'T HAVE. WHAT D'YOU SAY?"

"Well, he thinks he did," says Duck, "but he's wrong. He's been set-up. And I'm determined to prove it."

"CONVICTED OF A CRIME HE DIDN'T COMMIT? WE'VE ALL BEEN THERE," says RUSTY, who has gone back to exercising and is now doing something called "crunches". "YOU GOTTA NOTION WHO DID DO IT?"

"Yes, I think I do," says Duck, nodding. "I've gone over all the events and I've uncovered some very interesting evidence."

I has never heard Duck talk like this before. It's like he has become some super Duck-Detective.

"The first question I asked myself," he continues, "is how did Pig's mouth end up filled with **Ki-Ki's** feathers? A quick scout of the surrounding area revealed a large turnip-shaped hole in the veggie patch. I believe whoever really did do this removed said turnip and used it to get Pig to open his mouth. Pig can't resist turnips, not even in his sleep. The true culprit then posted the feathers into his mouth as he happily chomped away on it."

"PHANTOM FEEDING. AN OLD TRICK. AIN'T SEEN THAT ONE SINCE MY DAYS WITH SPECIAL FORCES," says **RUSTY** between his crunches.

"Then I went back over Pig's claim he was visited in the middle of the night by an old enemy. I thought this was impossible. But, a closer inspection of his house proved I was wrong. Sorry, Pig," says Duck, looking at me. "I found a small, secret hatch cut into the side of it, and most tellingly, I found footprints: thin, long, three-toed footprints. There's only one creature I know that has feet like that. EVIL CHICKENS!"

RUSTY suddenly stops his crunching and sits up. "EVIL CHICKENS, HUH? TELL ME MORE, SOLDIER Duck. I'M ALL EARS." What a strange thing to say — he only has two! It must be another special soldier saying.

"Well, that's about as far as I've got. I've no doubt the EVIL CHICKENS are behind all this," Duck says, "but there's one question I still don't have the answer to: if **Ki-Ki** isn't in Pig's tummy, exactly where is he?"

"YOU CAN GUARANTEE ONE THING," growls RUSTY, flashing his pointy teeth. "IF THE ECS ARE INVOLVED THE ANSWER AIN'T GONNA BE PRETTY. THOSE BIRDS PLAY DIRTY!"

"You has met them?" I asks, surprised to hear he has. I can't imagine how.

"I GOT HISTORY WITH THEIR KIND," he growls. "THAT'S ALL I'M SAYIN'. IF **CHICKENS** ARE INVOLVED, THEN THIS OLD DOG WANTS IN. ME AND THEM GOT SOME UNFINISHED BUSINESS."

"That's great news," says Duck. "We're going to need all the help we can get. If we can find them, then I am sure we can prove Pig is innocent, and hopefully find **Ki-Ki** too."

"AFFIRMATIVE, SOLDIER Duck. BUT WE NEED TO MOVE FAST. AS I SEE IT WE GOT OURSELVES TWO CHALLENGES HERE. NUMBER 1: WE GOTTA AVOID DEFRA — THEY AIN'T GONNA LET US JUST RUN AWAY LIKE THAT. NUMBER 2: WE GOTTA ASCERTAIN THE ENEMY POSITION. BUT WE AIN'T GONNA BE ABLE TO ADVANCE ON EITHER GOAL TILL WE GOT YOU SOLDIERS SOME BWST: BASIC WOODLAND SURVIVAL TRAININ'. STUFF'S ABOUT TO GET REAL. YOU READY FOR THAT? YOU READY TO LEAVE YOUR COMFORT ZONES?"

Me and **Duck** both looks at each other. I don't thinks either of us has any idea what he just said. But we both nods.

"THAT'S WHAT I LIKE TO HEAR, SOLDIERS," Rusty says. "LET'S GET BUSY."

Zero Rest Hours

Hello.

I, Soldier Pig, is VERY pleased to report that I is not going to starve! HOORAY!!! There may be no one to serve me slops in the woods, but there is food. Really tasty food.

RUSTY has shown me these amazing things called acorns. At first I is not sure about them; they smells like a mix of mouldy wood and wet earth. But then I takes a little bite and I discovers they is in fact little balls of delicious yumminess. **RUSTY** tells me these is what Pigs used to eat in the old days before they got soft and went and lived with **Farmers**. He says they is an NSN: Natural Source of Nutrition, and that wherever there is woods you can find them. AMAZING!!!!

"EAT UP," he says, "'COS YOU'RE GONNA NEED ALL THE ENERGY YOU GOT FOR WHAT I HAVE PLANNED NEXT."

He's not wrong. What he has planned is something he calls BCT: Basic Combat Training. (RUSTY likes to shorten things down to just letters.) At first I gets all excited. I imagines soon becoming a Brave Action Pig (a BAP — see, I can do it too!).

But then the training starts and it's not quite as fun as I'd hoped. I don't feel so

much like a BAP as a RAP (Rubbish Action
Pig). **Duck** seems to find it all much easier
than me, which is very annoying, and quite
unfair. I is bigger and stronger, surely I
should make a better soldier?!

"FIRST UP," barks RUSTY, "PHASE ONE:
ENEMY AVOIDANCE. WE GOTTA GET STEALTHY.
WE GOTTA LEARN TO 'TREAD SILENTLY'. THIS
APPLIES PARTICULARLY TO YOU, LEAD BOOTS,"
he says, looking straight at me. "WE NEED
YOU SOUNDIN' MORE 'LITTLE MOUSE' AND LESS
'MASSIVE MOOSE'."

He demonstrates a special way of walking.
I has to pick my feet really high up off
the ground, then place them back down
super softly. I feels like I is doing some silly

dance. **Duck** is lucky – he is so light that he hardly makes any noise as he walks, so he doesn't have to do any funny prancy-stepping. It takes me ages to just get the hang of making half the noise I normally does. The woodland floor is just too full of things what goes crunch and snap.

Next **RUSTY** tells us about burying our poo. He says this is very important in "combat situations". If you leave your poo lying around, it is easy to see where you has been. Before we does one, we has to dig a hole to do it into. Then, once we has finished, we has to fill the hole back in and pat the earth down to make it look like it never happened. Again, **Duck** is super lucky. His poo is tiny. He only has to dig a little hole. My poo is massive, so I has to dig a much bigger one. This is very tiring and takes ages. GRRRRRR!

Duck's poo

my poo

"**GOOD WORK, SOLDIERS,**" says **RUSTY**, nodding at where we has buried our poo. "**NOW, LET'S TAKE IT TO THE NEXT LEVEL. PHASE TWO: SURVIVAL TRAINING. GOTTA STAY ALIVE TO STAY IN THE GAME! TIME TO BUILD OURSELVES SOME BASIC SHELTERS: A PLACE TO HIDE, A PLACE TO REST.**"

RUSTY gathers some long branches and stands them up so they makes a tall, pointy triangle shape. He then lays twigs across them and covers them in bits of bracken and leaves.

"ONE WOODLAND SHELTER," he says, showing off what he has built.

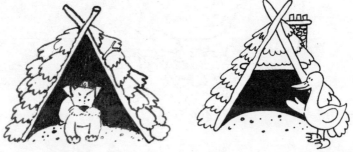

We both has a go at making one. I has to say I is quite pleased with mine until I sees **Duck's** — his is more perfect than **RUSTY'S** and has even got a little chimney. **Duck's** nest-building practice has given him a huge advantage. As **RUSTY** walks around looking at what we has made, a breeze blows through the trees and mine collapses.

"WELL, SOLDIER PIG," he says, **"THAT'S**

QUITE AN ACHIEVEMENT. YOU'VE SINGLE-
HANDEDLY INVENTED A SHELTER THAN TURNS
INTO A BED. QUITE SOME FEAT!"

I can't decide whether he means this as a
good thing or not.

"RIGHT, THE FINAL PHASE. PHASE THREE:
PHYSICAL EXERCISE. NO POINT HAVING SURVIVAL
SKILLS IF YOU AIN'T FIT ENOUGH TO SURVIVE," he
says, giving my tummy a firm pat. I tries

to hold it in and stop it wobbling around too much, but I is not very successful.

"DON'T YOU WORRY, SOLDIER PIG, WE'LL SOON HAVE THAT STOMACH SO FIRM YOU COULD BOUNCE ACORNS OFF IT!" he barks. "NOW, FIRST UP, SQUAT THRUSTS."

He gives us a demonstration. He balances on his two front paws and jumps back and forth on his back leg. He makes it look super easy. Not a problem, I thinks.

WRONG! I does two of them and is so tired I nearly collapses. All four of my legs feels like jelly – **RUSTY** has an unfair advantage having just three. **Duck** does ten like it is no bother at all. His body is really light. So unfair!

I tries to do another one. It hurts so much I can't help but let out a little moan.

"REMEMBER, SOLDIER, PAIN'S JUST WEAKNESS LEAVING THE BODY," says RUSTY loudly in my ear.

He's wrong. I feels full of pain and none of it seems to be leaving.

"NOW, SIT-UPS," he says. "GET DOWN AND GIVE ME TWENTY."

Duck gives his wings a little flex, then lies down on his back. He curls his wings around behind his head, then lifts it up and touches his beak to his feet. I stares in amazement – how does **Duck** know about all this stuff? Does he do a secret workout in his **Duck House** every morning?

I gets down and does my best to copy, only I has a big fat belly in-between my head and my toes — it's almost impossible. All the air in my body gets squashed into the middle. Instead of doing a sit-up, I does an enormous fart. It's unlike any I has ever done before. It doesn't make a sound, not even a little hiss. The only way you would know that I has done it is because the air suddenly fills with a strong acorny pong. It's REALLY stinky. I is so happy. My farts no longer smell of flowers.

"SNF: SILENT NINJA FARTING. I LIKE IT," says RUSTY, giving me a pat on the bottom. "BET YOUR ANCESTORS USED THAT TO GREAT EFFECT."

"What does you mean?" I asks, hoping he is going to tell me about some great fart games what old Pigs used to play.

"I MEAN IT WOULD HAVE AFFORDED THEM THE ELEMENT OF SURPRISE WHEN THEY SNUCK UP ON THEIR PREY. I RECKON FARTS LIKE THAT COULD DO SERIOUS DAMAGE IF USED CORRECTLY — COULD KNOCK A SMALL CREATURE OUT AT TWENTY PACES, OR AT LEAST MAKE IT SO SICK IT COULDN'T MOVE. GOOD JOB THE WIND'S NOT BLOWING IN SOLDIER Duck's DIRECTION. REMEMBER, LIKE I SAID, YOU PIGS GOT THAT

OMNIVORE THING GOING ON! IT AIN'T CARROTS YOUR ANCESTORS WAS HUNTIN'."

I wish he would stop mentioning the Omnivore thing. I is really trying as hard as I can to believe that I DIDN'T eat **Ki-Ki**.

"RIGHT, SOLDIERS!" Rusty says, changing the subject. **"THINK IT'S TIME WE PUT OUR NEW SKILLS TO WORK IN THE FIELD. YOU FEEL RFSA: READY FOR SOME ACTION?"**

I has to say, I feels RFABLD: Ready For a Big Lie-Down, but I doesn't think that is the sort of thing a soldier should be saying or doing.

Contact! Contact!

Hello.

I is so pleased to be writing this, because it means that it is the end of the day and oh, what a day it has been!!!

Immediately after our training finishes we "strikes camp". This means knocking down everything we has built and covering up everything we has done, or made. I likes this bit – I is good at knocking stuff over. Just to be on the safe side I also gobbles – I means clears up – every acorn I can find too.

Whilst we does this **RUSTY** disappears off into the woods. When he comes back he is covered in stripes of brown and green.

"BEFORE WE PROCEED," says RUSTY, beckoning us over, "THERE IS JUST ONE LAST SMALL MATTER WE NEED TO TACKLE. SOLDIER PIG, YOU'RE TOO PINK. SOLDIER Duck, YOU'RE TOO WHITE. WE GOTTA BLEND YOU INTO THE WOODS BETTER. TIME TO GET YOU TWO CAMOED UP."

RUSTY shows us what he means. We has to smear ourselves all over with earth, moss and leaves. There is a lot of me to cover, so RUSTY gives me some help. Soon I looks just like him. I looks down at myself. It's amazing; the green and brown stripes really does make us blend in. It's like I is sort-of almost invisible.

"THAT'S BETTER!" says RUSTY, inspecting us. "IF I SQUINT IT'S LIKE NEITHER OF YOU ARE THERE. HA! HA!"

I laughs along with him, but **Duck** doesn't seem to find it so funny. I likes being all dirty, but I is not so sure he does — when he is on the **Farm** he always keeps his feathers nice and clean.

"OK," continues RUSTY, "TIME TO MOVE OUT. I WANT YOU TO MAINTAIN A CONSTANT STATE OF SUSPICIOUS ALERTNESS AT ALL TIMES. IF WE'RE GONNA FIND THESE ENEMY **CHICKENS**

WE GOTTA NOT GET OURSELVES CAUGHT. I'LL LEAD. Duck, YOU TAKE THE MIDDLE. PIG, YOU BRING UP THE REAR. LET'S GO."

I likes "BRINGING UP THE REAR" – it means I can stop and eat acorns without **Duck** or **RUSTY** noticing. I has a little nibble, then I quickly catches them back up before they has time to realize what I is doing.

I has just catched up with them for the fourth time, after finding and eating the biggest acorn yet (it was nearly the size of a Brussels sprout!), when we reaches the edge of a small stream. All of a sudden **RUSTY** holds his paw up in the air and stops still as a statue. **Duck** immediately freezes too. I tries to freeze, but I is mid-jog so I ends up in a really difficult position. My front leg is halfway off the ground and so is one of my back ones. It takes all my balancing powers not to fall over. I really hopes we doesn't have to stand like this for too long.

RUSTY signals at something up ahead. I looks at where he is pointing. Through the trees I sees a path and on the path I sees a bench. Sitting on it is a **Farmer**! She's reading a newspaper — I knows what these is as **Mr Sandal** sometimes sits in his veggie-patch chair reading one.

I can just make out the picture on the front of it.

It looks like a Pig.

It looks a lot like a Pig like me.

In fact ... I THINKS IT IS ME!!!!

I lets out a little gasp. **RUSTY** and **Duck** both turns around and gives me a "**Shhhhhh!**" stare. Being stared at makes my balancing go all wrong and, with a loud splosh, I stumbles head first into the stream. The water is freezing cold. I pulls myself out as quick as I can.

The **Farmer** looks up. She stares straight through the woods towards where I is standing. For a moment I hopes my camo will stop her seeing me. But then I catches a glimpse of my reflection. The water from the stream has smudged all the stripes. I looks like some sort of very ill, green-monster Pig.

"**AHHHHHHHHHHHHHH!**" she screams, dropping the paper and running off down the path, her **Farmer** arms flapping like a crazy bird's.

"**CONTACT. WAIT OUT,**" whispers **RUSTY**, crouching down. **Duck** and I both copies him. We waits until we is sure the **Farmer** has gone, then **RUSTY** runs over and grabs the newspaper and brings it back. I stares down at the Pig picture. I was right, it is me. **Mr and Mrs Sandal** must have taken it without me knowing – it is a picture of me eating a turnip. I looks very happy.

"**DANGEROUS PIG ON THE RUN**," says **Duck**, reading the **Farmer** words underneath it. "**A diseased Pig is on the run in the local woods. The creature, who is highly aggressive, should not be approached. Anyone who sees it is advised to keep well clear and contact DEFRA immediately.**"

I can't believe I is on the front of the

newspaper. I wishes it was about doing something good so that I could be proud.

RUSTY suddenly goes super-still again. His ears prick up and he sniffs the air.

"**DEFRA**," he whispers, "**INCOMING FROM THE EAST. THEY MUST HAVE FOLLOWED THE SOUND OF SCREAMING.**"

I looks around. I can't see them.

"**ETA ONE MINUTE AND COUNTING**," he continues. "**SOLDIER Duck, USING YOUR HOMING SKILLS, CAN YOU DETERMINE THE DIRECTION OF THE Farm?**"

"Affirmative. Latitude: three zero degrees one four decimal five minutes by longitude: zero eight degrees one eight decimal three minutes."

Wow! **Duck** just keeps on surprising me

with the things he can do and knows. I really is going to have to have a long chat with him if I survives all this. I looks behind; in the distance I sees a flash of white moving between the trees. Deathra! **RUSTY'S** nose was right.

"**QUICK, SOLDIERS! THIS WAY**," he barks, dashing across the path and into the woods on the other side.

Duck is surprisingly fast; he can almost keep up with **RUSTY**. Dodging around brambles and bushes is definitely easier when you is smaller, and maybe when you has not been filling yourself up on delicious acorns all morning — oooopsie.

"**COME ON, SOLDIER PIG!**" **RUSTY** shouts back

at me. "**WE AIN'T OUT ON SOME SUNDAY AFTERNOON STROLL IN THE PARK!**" I tries to speed up but my legs  keep bashing against my acorn-filled tummy as it swings around.

I hears a loud, nasty hiss close behind me. I glances over my shoulder. It's Deathra — they is getting closer with every step.

"SHHHHHHTAB SHHHHIM WISHHHHHH SHHORE SHHHHTICK," I hears Big Deathra hiss. I has no idea what he has said, but I soon gets a pretty good idea what he means.

I hears the buzz of the electric stick

being turned on. The thought of it makes my legs go all wibbly-wobbly. I stumbles forward – I tries to stop myself falling but I can't.

I tumbles over head first and before I knows it – BUMPH! BUMPH! BUMPH! – I is bouncing down a steep slope and into a tangly pile of bushes.

"PIG !!!"

I hears **Duck** cry out.

I looks up; scrambling down towards me is Deathra. I rolls over and tries to run, but my front leg gets tangled up in some ivy. I falls flat on my face.

"HSSSSSS, HSSSSSS, HSSSSSSS!" they both laughs through their helmets.

Small Deathra lurches towards me with the electric stick.

"NO! PLEASE, NOOOOOOO!!" I screams.

He's just about to stab it into my bottom when I hears a familiar cry:

"YIPPEE-KI-YAY!!!!!!!!" howls **RUSTY**, leaping through the air and biting on to Little Deathra's bottom.

Little Deathra cries out, swinging around to try and see what's causing his pain. As he does he by mistake hits Big Deathra in

the belly with his electric stick. Blue sparks
fly out. Big Deathra falls to the floor
clutching his middle and groaning.

RUSTY drops to the ground. Little
Deathra angrily lunges at him. Only as he
does he trips over one of Big Deathra's
large feet. He falls forwards, landing
on top of his buzzing stick. His body
judders around like he's being stung
by a thousand bees.

Duck rushes over and frees my
leg.

"**COME ON!**" shouts **RUSTY**. "**THEY'RE
DOWN, BUT NOT FOR LONG.**"

Now I has seen how painful being
stabbed with the electric stick

REALLY is, I finds that I can run quite a
bit faster. I can almost keep up.

The woods is huge. It feels like we runs
for a million miles. I starts to wonder if
we is ever going to stop, but finally, I is
pleased to say
we does.

RUSTY holds up his paw and sniffs the air.

"Has ... we ... lost ... them?" I manages to splutter out. My chest feels so tight, like **COW** is sitting on it.

"AFFIRMATIVE, SOLDER PIG." he says. "WE MUST HAVE REALLY COMPROMISED THEM BACK THERE. I DON'T THINK WE'LL BE SEEING THEM AGAIN TODAY."

I collapses to the floor. I knows it's probably not what a soldier is supposed to do, but I can't help it. I is completely and totally exhausted. I stares up through the trees. The sky is starting to get dark.

"OK, SOLDIERS. I THINK THAT'S ENOUGH ADVENTURE FOR ONE DAY," says **RUSTY**. "I SAY

WE MAKE CAMP HERE. GET SOME R&R – REST AND RECUPERATION – AND CRACK ON FIRST THING IN THE AM.".

Right now, I thinks these might be the best words I has ever heard anyone say. I don't thinks I has ever been so pleased for a day to be over!

Foxtrot Oscar X-Ray

Hello.

When I said the day was over I was wrong. It turns out there was still a tiny bit more to go. But I is not going to complain. Tonight we found out what **RUSTY** calls IBI: Important Breakthrough Intelligence.

RUSTY said he thought it best that he and **Duck** build our shelter and that I should use my hunting expertize to find leaves and bracken to make us a bed. I is not knowing that I has such skills; **RUSTY** must know things about me that even I doesn't.

Just as I is expertly gathering up a

really big bunch of leaves, I catches
something out of the corner
of my eye. Something
moving through the
woods. At first I
panics — what if it's
Deathra? But it's too
small and the wrong
shape.

"**You!!!!**" says **Duck** angrily, putting down
the twigs he was building with and turning to
face the creature. I can see it more clearly
now. Its sharp face and yellow eyes is becoming
clearer as it comes out of the shadows.

"**WELL, WELL, WELL, FOXTROT, OSCAR, X-RAY,**"
says **RUSTY**.

"**FOX!**" says **Duck**. He almost spits the word out.

FOX! **FOX** WILL EAT **DUCK**!! JUST LIKE HE ATE ALL HIS FAMILY!!! I runs around and stands myself between **Duck** and nasty, nasty, **Fox**.

"Back off!" I shouts. "I is an Omnivore – you know what that means? It means, if I wants, I could eat you up. And if you so much as lays one paw on **Duck**, I will!"

"**Ah, Pig!**" says **Fox** in a voice that totally surprises me. I has never actually heard him speak. I imagined he would sound nasty, like he looks. But his voice is soft and sounds more like he is singing than talking. "**Cool your trotters, boyo. No need to be coming over all unnecessary-like. I'm keepin' it tidy these days. No fatty proteins or carbs after six o'clock, and I has to say I feels all the better for it. It's given me so much more energy.**"

"**Fatty proteins!**" I hears **Duck** mutter under his breath. "**Is that all my family was to you?**"

"**You should try it; it's all the rage up in the valleys,**" continues **Fox**, who is clearly not hearing **Duck**, or is just ignoring him. "**Now tell me, what's occurin'? What brings you to my patch? You're not here to talk healthy eating now, are you?**"

"**WE'RE LOOKING FOR SOME OLD ACQUAINTANCES**," says **RUSTY**, circling him and giving him a good sniff. "**SOME CHICKENS. WOULDN'T HAPPEN TO HAVE COME ACROSS ANY WOULD YOU? SMELLS LIKE YOU MIGHT'VE.**"

"**Ah! An ol' DOG'S intuition,**" says **Fox**, his yellow eyes twinkling in the moonlight. "**You're right. As it goes I have seen them. And I'd wager I've a pretty good idea why you're lookin' for them too. I heard what happened to you in that henhouse sounded pretty** immense. *And I don't mean in a good way neither."*

"NOW, YOU KNOW THE RULES, *Fox*," says RUSTY firmly. "WHAT HAPPENS IN THE HENHOUSE, STAYS IN THE HENHOUSE. WE BOTH KNOW THAT."

"Fair play, fair play!" nods *Fox.* *"Well you've caught me in a good mood – must be another positive effect of the new diet – so I'll tell you what I know. You'll find what you're looking for up the Old Oak Tree. I've no idea what they're up to, mind. You know those crafty birds – always up to some shenanigans or other."*

"If you knows where they is, why hasn't you eaten them? How do we know you is not trying to trick us?" I says, not sure whether to believe him or not. I knows how much **FOX** loves **CHICKENS**. He was always trying to get into the **CHICKEN HOUSE** and eat them when they lived on the **Farm**. I can't understand why he wouldn't be gobbling them up now he has the chance.

"*I won't lie to you – I do favour the fowl. White meat is so much easier on the stomach than red,*" he says, looking over at **Duck** and smiling. "*But honestly, they've offered me a crackin' little deal: I leave them alone and they say they'll make all my Christmases come at once. They've promised me something proper tasty if I keep my distance.*"

"WELL, IT SURE SOUNDS LIKE YOU GOT YOURSELF AN INTERESTING PROPOSITION THERE," replies RUSTY. "THANKS FOR THE HEADS-UP."

"*Always a pleasure*," says **Fox**, turning his twinkling yellow eyes on to **Duck**. "*And I do hope our paths cross again – preferably pre six o'clock. It would be so nice to complete the set, if you catch my drift ...*"

"If you think I'm even going to grace your puerile, childish goading with an answer," snarls **Duck**, his beak clenched so tightly the words can hardly get out, "**then you can think again.**"

"*OK! OK! No need to get all hot 'n' bothered. I'm only jokin' ...*" laughs **Fox**, turning and disappearing back into the woods.

"*... Or am I? Ha! Ha! Ha!*" His voice echoes back out of the darkness: "**or ... am ... I?**"

Ha! Ha! Ha!

"Wow, **Duck!**" I says. "I can't believe, after all he has done, you isn't super scared of him."

"**He may have taken my family,**" says **Duck**, picking up a twig and snapping it angrily in half, "**but I'll never let him take my dignity!**"

Clear and Present Danger

Hello.

I is happy to say that once again I has woken up and has not eaten anyone. In fact last night I slept very well. I thinks this is partly because **RUSTY** and **Duck** built such a good shelter, but mainly because of my expert bed gathering and making.

When I wakes up I finds that **RUSTY** has gathered a pile of acorns for me and some worms for **Duck**. I doesn't like to think what he might have eaten himself — I knows that **DOGS** is not Vegytarians.

"EAT UP, SOLDIERS," he says. **"THE THEATRE OF WAR IS NO PLACE FOR THE WEAK. OUR FIRST**

OBJECTIVE OF THE DAY: REACH THE OLD OAK TREE AND CONFIRM PRESENCE OF ENEMY CHICKEN."

Duck and I nods in agreement. We gobbles up our food, strikes our camp, reapplies the camo what got washed off me yesterday, and sets off towards the Old Oak Tree. **Duck** knows the way so he leads.

RUSTY says today is what **Farmers** call "Sunday". This means Deathra won't be working; Sunday is a special day when **Farmers** is allowed to be lazy. So he says we can "**FOCUS ALL OUR ATTENTION ON THE FORWARD ENEMY POSITION, WITHOUT FEAR OF COMPROMISE FROM BEHIND.**" Phew! I doesn't want anything bad to happen to my behind. Ha! Ha! Ha!

Duck leads us back to the edge of the **Farm**. As soon as I glimpses it through the trees, my heart starts to fill up with sad feelings. Even though it has been fun meeting **RUSTY** and learning lots of bonkers stuff, I can't help but wish I was back there. Back playing **where's woc?** with **COW**, Name That Fart with **Duck** and watching **Ki-Ki** make his strange jewellery.

I spots Mrs Jingle Jangle. She is sitting all alone on the step of her van. In her hand I can just make out something long and thin — it's one of **Ki-Ki's** feathers. She brushes it against the side of her face. Though I can't hear from this far away, I is pretty sure she's crying.

I so wishes everything could just go back to the way it was before.

I lets out a sad little Piggy sigh, what no one is meant to hear. But of course **RUSTY** and his super-duper hearing does.

"**YOU SMELL THEM TOO, SOLDIER PIG?**" he whispers. "**OF COURSE YOU DO. EC'S HAVE A SMELL NO ONE CAN FORGET.**"

I nods. But I can't smell anything but trees.

"**SOLDIERS. PROCEED FORWARD WITH CAUTION.**

CHICKENS HAVE THREE-HUNDRED DEGREE VISION. WE DON'T WANT TO BE SPOTTED," he says. **"TIME TO EMPLOY SOME 'SOFT TREADING'."**

I does my very best prancy-stepping. My soldier-ness must be improving; I makes much less noise than I did in training. A little way before we reaches the tree **RUSTY** holds up his paw and stops us. He makes some funny motions. He taps himself on the top of his head, makes a digging motion, then points at his eyes. It's like he's doing some strange dance with no music.

"We're going to dig in here and observe from a safe distance," whispers **Duck,** translating for me.

This literally means we dig a big hole and

sits in it. Well, the hole wouldn't have to be so big if I didn't have to fit in it too. Luckily **RUSTY** is a very fast digger and I is not too bad either. My nose makes a very good shovel.

Once the hole is finished we gets in and begins our "observation phase". **Duck** is too short to see over the top, so I lets him sit on my shoulders. I knows this may still not be 100% safe, but I is still feeling full after this morning's acorns.

I stares over at the Old Oak Tree. It looks just like it always has, big and leafy. I can't see any sign of the **EVIL CHICKENS**. I starts to feel like maybe we was wrong to have believed **FOX**. Wrong to have believed that the **EVIL CHICKENS** is back and is having anything to do with **Ki-Ki** disappearing.

But then a strong breeze blows and rustles all the leaves and I catches a glimpse of something hanging from a branch. It looks like a little ladder.

I follows the ladder up. It goes to a small platform.

The breeze blows again, this time revealing even more.

The top of the tree is full of little platforms, and standing on them I can clearly make out some pointy shapes moving around.

POINTY EVIL CHICKEN SHAPES!!!!!

"I can see them, I can see them!" I whispers, pointing towards the top of the tree. "There, there! They really is back!!!"

"THEY SURE ARE, SOLDIER," growls **RUSTY**.

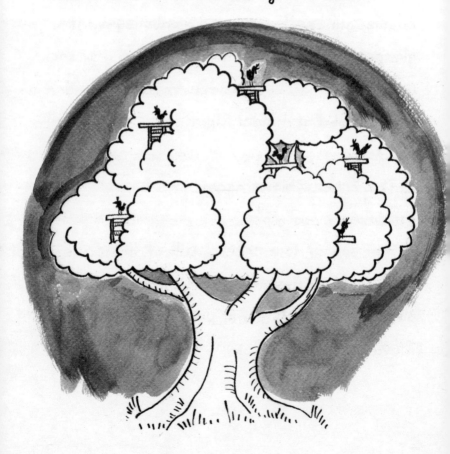

I notices as he speaks he digs his claws into the earth around the top of our hole. He digs them in so hard I is sure I actually see his paws shake. "**THEY SURE ARE!**" he growls again.

I looks back at the tree. Now I knows where to look I has no trouble spotting them. One of the platforms is much higher up than the others. Before I even sees it I knows who will be standing there. THE **SUPER EVIL CHICKEN**.

It stands proudly on its platform like it's the most important thing in the whole world. It lets out a loud cluck. All the others stand to attention. The **SUPER EVIL CHICKEN** swings itself off its platform and, using the little rope ladders what hangs between each one, makes its way down to a long, narrow plank of wood what is nailed to the top of the trunk.

On the plank stands a lone **CHICKEN**. Even from this distance, by the way it moves, I can tell it's a particularly nasty one. It salutes the **SUPER EVIL CHICKEN** and draws a branch back to show it something round and feathery what is tied to the tree.

"**IS THAT WHAT I THINK IT IS???**" whispers **RUSTY**.

I squints hard. The feathery ball is tied up tightly with lots of rope and has a rag tied around its eyes so it can't see.

The **SUPER EVIL CHICKEN** pulls the rag down. I lets out a loud gasp. **Duck** reaches around and covers my mouth.

I can't believe what I is seeing.

"IT'S **KI-KI**!!!" I excitedly whispers through **Duck's** wing. "IT'S **KI-KI**!!!! He's not in my tummy. He's up the Old Oak Tree!"

"At last the concrete proof we need," says **Duck**, letting out a sigh of relief. **"Pig, you are innocent!"**

I DIDN'T EAT **KI-KI**! HOORAY!!! HOORAY!!!! This might be the best news I has ever had. In fact I is pretty sure it is — the only thing that'd be better would be to find out I didn't eat him whilst at the same time eating a turnip-sized acorn.

I wants to give **Duck** a huge big hug for being so right. But there isn't enough room in our hole and I is not sure that soldiers is meant to do hugging.

I takes another look at **Ki-Ki**, still not sure I can believe my eyes. My happy heart starts to sink. He may be alive, but he looks terrible. Now I knows where they got the feathers to put in my mouth; poor **Ki-Ki** is covered in little bald patches. I don't think they has been feeding him either — he looks much thinner than I remembers. His body is all droopy; the only thing that is holding him up is the ropes what ties him to the tree.

He lifts his head and mumbles something. I can't hear what he says, but **RUSTY'S** amazing ears does.

"HE SAYS THIS OUTDOOR LIVING IS PLAYING HAVOC WITH HIS COMPLEXION, THAT HIS PORES ARE ALL CLOGGED WITH DIRT AND THAT HE DESPERATELY NEEDS TO EXFOLIATE," whispers **RUSTY**, looking rather confused.

The **SUPER EVIL CHICKEN** lets out a nasty, loud laugh and tugs the rag back up over his eyes. **Ki-Ki's** poor head flops back down.

"So that's who they're bribing Fox with," says **Duck**, shaking his head.

"No!" I blurts out. "We can't let this happen. We has to stop them. I can't discover I didn't eat **Ki-Ki**, only for the **EVIL CHICKENS** to feed him to **Fox**!!!"

"DON'T YOU WORRY; WE'LL BUST OUT THE TURKEY ALL IN GOOD TIME. BUT FIRST WE GOTTA GET TO THE BOTTOM OF SOMETHING MUCH BIGGER," says RUSTY, turning to **Duck**. "I DON'T KNOW ABOUT YOU, BUT SOMETHING HERE DOESN'T ADD UP. IF THEY CAME BACK SOLELY TO TERMINATE SOLDIER PIG, HOW COME THEY'RE STILL HERE? WHY'VE THEY GONE TO ALL THE EFFORT OF BUILDING SUCH AN ELABORATE STRUCTURE IN THE TREE? AND WHY ARE THEY BRIBING **Fox** TO STAY AWAY? THIS WHOLE THING SMELLS VERY FISHY TO ME."

I don't get it. First **Duck** can smell fish, now **RUSTY**. I've got a bigger nose than both of them — how come I can't smell fish too?

E.E.G. (Evil Evidence Gathered)

Hello.

The **EVIL CHICKENS** is more evil than I thinks it is ever possible to be. Honestly, you couldn't make stuff like this up. Even if you were the world's best maker-upper.

The one thing the **EVIL CHICKENS** is not good at though is flying. To get down from the tree they has made this special platform what they lowers themselves to the floor on — they can then pull themselves up on it when they wants to go back up.

We watches as they all comes down,

the **SUPER EVIL CHICKEN** squawks some instructions and they all marches off towards the **Farm**.

"OK!" says RUSTY. "TIME FOR A LITTLE LIGHT RECONNAISSANCE!"

"He means we follow them to see what they are up to," whispers **Duck** helpfully in my ear.

"JUST ONE THING WE GOTTA ADDRESS BEFORE WE SHIP OUT: WOODLAND CAMO WORKS IN THE WOODS, BUT IT AIN'T GONNA CUT IT IN THE YARD. WE GOTTA HAVE A LITTLE WASH AND BRUSH UP."

"But if we just looks like us, doesn't we have more chance of being spotted?" I asks. I quite likes being covered in dirt.

"NEGATIVE, SOLDIER PIG. YOU LOOK LIKE A FOREST, AND I DON'T SEE NO FORESTS IN

THE YARD! IT'S TIME TO USE THE SKILLS I'VE
TAUGHT YOU. YOU CAN FART LIKE A NINJA, NOW
IT'S TIME TO ACT LIKE ONE!"

So, before we heads to the yard, we
sneaks over to the **Sheeps'** Pond and washes
the dirt off.

We has to be careful to avoid the **Sheeps**
— we doesn't want them to start shouting
"CARNIVAAAR" again and alerting the **EVIL
CHICKENS** or Mrs Jingle Jangle that we is coming.
Luckily they is over in the corner itching
themselves on the remains of the Trocket
what me and **Duck** crashed there a while ago.

Once we are all clean **RUSTY** takes a stick
and starts to draw a map of the **Farm**
in the mud.

"RIGHT, LISTEN IN, SOLDIERS. I SAY WE ENTER THE **Farm** HERE," he says, pointing at a place on his mud-map, "THROUGH THIS GATE. THEN, USING THE OLD BARN AS COVER, WE MOVE AROUND TO HERE - THE **COW'S** SHED. SHE'S A FRIENDLY, RIGHT?"

"Yes, lovely," I says, "very friendly."

"OK, WE'LL USE HER SHED TO ASCERTAIN THE ENEMY POSITION. THEN WE'LL PLAN FURTHER. RIGHT, FALL IN BEHIND ME. AND REMEMBER: STEALTH! STEALTH! STEALTH!"

We carefully creeps over to the gate. **RUSTY** quietly opens it, looks around and then makes a quick dash to the Old Barn. He presses himself up against it and signals for us to follow. **Duck** and I dashes across and lines ourselves up next to him.

"OK," he whispers, "WE ONLY GOT A SHORT DISTANCE TO GET TO THE **COW**. BUT IT'S OPEN GROUND. WE'RE GONNA BE IN PLAIN SIGHT. YOU'RE GONNA NEED TO KEEP YOUR WITS ABOUT YOU, SOLDIERS!"

I is not sure what "wits" is, and I is even more sure I doesn't have any to keep with me. **Duck** nods, so I guesses he must have some. I decides to pretend I does too.

We creeps to the edge of the Old Barn and peers around it. I can see **COW** in her shed. She is busy eating some hay. I is so pleased to see her; I has really missed her and her funny words.

RUSTY sniffs the air and then makes a dash across to her shed. Once he is safely behind it he signals to us. **Duck** goes next; I has to say he does look very funny when he waddles so fast.

Finally it's my turn. I takes a deep breath and, doing my very best "soft stepping", runs as fast as I can towards them. But just as I is halfway across I hears the door to Mrs Jingle Jangle's van open. **RUSTY** signals for me to get down. I presses myself as flat as I can against the ground.

I peeks across to see what Mrs Jingle Jangle is doing. She is standing at the door carrying a large basket of very colourful washing. It's piled up so high that I can't see her face, which I really hopes means she can't see mine. I can hear her voice though. She is singing a slow song.

She carefully starts to walk down the

steps of her van. The problem is that as she steps down, the basket gets lower and her head gets higher. Any minute now I is sure her eyes is going to rise above it and she is going to spot me.

"Oh, my Moonstone," I hears her sing, "how I miss you-ooh-oooh. Feels like my heart has broken in two-ooo-oooh."

I knows this is not a happy song, even though I only understands the word "Moonstone". I presses myself even harder into the ground. I looks over at **RUSTY**. I can tell from the look in his eyes he is as worried as I is.

She's going to spot me and call Deathra again!

My heart starts beating so loudly it's all I can hear.

BOOM! BOOM! BOOM! it goes. BOOM! BOOM! BRRRRING! BRRRRING! BRRRRING! BRRRRRING!

That's funny, I thinks, what's going on inside me? But then I realizes the sound is not coming from inside me, it's coming from inside Mrs Jingle Jangle's van. I looks across just in time to see her put down her washing basket and go back inside.

RUSTY frantically signals for me to get up. I scrambles to my feet and, forgetting all my ninja-ness, runs over to him and **Duck**.

"PHEW!" he says. "SAVED BY THE BELL. 'EY, SOLDIER PIG. GOOD JOB HER PHONE RANG!"

I has no idea what a phone is, I is just
so happy that it did whatever it did and
I wasn't spotted. I lets out possibly the
longest sigh of relief I has ever done.

"**god???**" I hears **COW'S** voice
say. I looks up and there she is,
gazing down at **RUSTY**,
looking very confused.

"**MORNIN' MA'AM,**" says
RUSTY, politely saluting her.

"**DOG,**" I says. She really does have the
funniest way of getting her words the
wrong way round.

"**pig!**" she cries. "**licker pig!!!!**"

"**He's no killer, COW. We've got proof!**"
whispers **Duck**.

"AFFIRMATIVE, MA'AM. WE HAVE VERIFIED COUNTER-INTELLIGENCE. SOLDIER PIG IS IN THE CLEAR," continues RUSTY. "BUT NOW WE HAVE ANOTHER ESCALATING SITUATION WE NEED TO GET TO THE BOTTOM OF. A CODE RED. WE NEED TO REPURPOSE YOUR SHED AS A HIDEOUT."

"roger that!" says COW. I can't believe it. First Duck, now COW! How does they both know all this soldier stuff?

We all tucks into COW'S shed. It's a bit of a squeeze — the shed is only really big enough for her. Duck hops up on to her back so he can get a clear view of the yard over her gate.

"I have eyes on the enemy," he whispers down to us. "They've all gathered in Pig House."

"WHAT! How dare they? First they makes it look like I is eating **Ki-Ki** Now they is taking over my house!

"**green potatoes!!!!**" says **COW**. Green potatoes means VERY BAD in Pig; they can make us extremely sick.

"**They're having a meeting,**" says **Duck**, "**but we're too far away for me to clearly hear what they are saying. Can you, RUSTY?**"

RUSTY pricks up his ears. "**NEGATIVE, I'M PICKING UP TOO MUCH BACKGROUND NOISE. NO PROBLEM, THOUGH. I'VE GOT AN IDEA.**" Quick as a flash he dashes over to the **Sandals'** shed. A couple of minutes later he returns carrying two plastic flowerpots tied together with a long piece of string. He sneaks over

157

to my house and quietly slips one
of the flowerpots underneath
my door. He brings the other
one back to us.

"**ear listener!**" says **COW**
excitedly. She's right. Through the flowerpot
we can clearly hear everything the **EVIL
CHICKENS** is saying. AMAZING. We all
gathers around and listens.

"**HOW'S YOUR FOWL, SOLDIERS?**" says **RUSTY**.
"**I AIN'T HEARD IT SPOKEN IN A VERY LONG TIME.**"

I tells him I doesn't speak or understand it.

"**No problem. I'll translate,**" says **Duck**.
The **SUPER EVIL CHICKEN** clears its throat
and begins to talk. **Duck** repeats back all
it says.

"FELLOW CHICKENS, OUR JOURNEY HERE HAS BEEN A LONG ONE. FIRST WE WERE UNJUSTLY ROCKETED INTO SPACE BY THAT RIDICULOUSLY SMELLY, FAT LUMP OF A CREATURE THEY CALL A PIG."

"KLA! KLA! KLA! SILLY, STINKY PIG!" the rest all chants.

"BUT, THANKS TO CHICKEN SIX'S BRAVE, FIERY SACRIFICE, WE CHANGED THE TRAJECTORY OF THE ROCKET-SHED HE SENT US OFF IN, AND MADE IT BACK DOWN HERE TO EARTH."

"HUZZAH, CHICKEN SIX! WE'LL NEVER FORGET YOU!" they all cheer.

"AND OF COURSE, LET'S NOT FORGET

CHICKEN FIVE AND CHICKEN EIGHT. WITHOUT THEM WE WOULD NEVER HAVE BEEN ABLE TO KEEP THE FARMERS FROM EATING US, LET ALONE STUFF THEM SO FULL OF EGGS THAT WE COULD ROLL THEM OUT OVER THE OCEAN WHILE THEY WERE SLEEPING."

Huzzah Chicken Six!

"FIVE AND EIGHT! HUZZAH! HURRAH!" they all cheer again.

The mention of the **Farmers** sends a shiver down my back. I will never forget the day I found out they wanted to eat me.

Duck continues to translate:

"NOW, FRIENDS, WITH OLD FARTY PANTS FINALLY TAKEN CARE OF..."

"KLA! KLA! KLA!" they all laugh evily.

"...IT IS TIME TO MOVE ON TO THE SECOND AND FINAL PHASE OF OUR MASTER PLAN. THIS I CALL, 'ADIOS, OLD LADY, BYE, BYE, OLD BIDDY, GOODBYE, GRANDMA'. YES, WE 'REMOVE' THE NEW Farmer AND INSTALL OUR SUPERIOR SELVES AS OWNERS. WE SHALL THEN BE FREE TO DO AS WE PLEASE: EAT EVERYONE'S FOOD, REFUSE TO LAY ANOTHER EGG, POO AS MUCH AS WE WANT ON THE COW AND LIVE THE ROYAL LIFE WE DESERVE. SOON MY DEAR FRIENDS, ALL THIS WILL BE OURS, THIS IS OUR FUTURE, AND

NOBODY CAN STOP US! KLA! KLA! KLA!"

COW lets out an angry snort. I knows how much she hated it when the **EVIL CHICKENS** used to roost on her back and then poo on it. Who wouldn't?!

"**IN THIS STINKING FILTH PIT OF A SHED,**" continues **Duck**, listening intently to the flowerpot, "**WE HAVE EVERYTHING WE NEED TO SEE THE BATTY OLD BEAN, AND HER RIDICULOUS OVER-PAINTED WACKY-WAGON, OFF INTO THE SKY. I AND MY NUMBER TWO HAVE SPENT A LOT OF TIME PREPARING A MOST MAGNIFICENT PLAN. COMRADE NUMBER TWO, WOULD YOU NOW PLEASE EXPLAIN WHY WE HAVE BROUGHT EVERYONE HERE TODAY AND WHAT THEY ARE REQUIRED**

TO DO?"

Number Two explains to the rest how they is going to fetch lumps of my old fermented poo — what is round the back of my house — and then along with a battery, which they is going to steal from the radio in **Mrs and Mrs Sandals'** shed, build a turbocharged bomb. Once they has made it, they

is going to pop it under Mrs Jingle Jangle's van and then, using a "remote wire", "detonate it" from the safety of my house.

"**WE WANT THE BOMB BUILT BY THE END OF THE DAY!**" Number Two tells the rest. "**WE WANT IT READY AND PRIMED TO BLOW HER AWAY TOMORROW MORNING, AROUND BREAKFAST TIME. WE CALCULATE THAT AROUND THIS TIME SHE WILL BE TOO ENGROSSED IN WHATEVER ORGANIC WIND-DRIED GRANOLA NONSENSE SHE EATS TO NOTICE US PLANTING IT.**"

Just as Number Two's speech finishes, and all the **EVIL CHICKENS** sets about their task, the door of Mrs Jingle Jangle's

van opens and
she comes out
with her big
basket of
washing again.
She struggles
across to the washing
line with it. She
looks older than I
remembers; her face looks tired and sad.
As she hangs up her washing she continues
singing her sad Moonstone song.

First of all she loses her cat, then she
loses **Ki-Ki**, and now she is about to be
blown up by the crazy **EVIL CHICKENS**!
Poor, poor Mrs Jingle Jangle.

I so wish I had learnt about burying my poo before. That way the **EVIL CHICKENS** would never have been able to build their horrible Pig Poo Bomb. Their Pomb. This is the second time I has made up a word that doesn't make me laugh. I thinks I might stop with the word making-up thing until all this is over!

"We has to stop them — we has to stop them right now!" I says.

"COOL YOUR JETS, SOLDIER PIG. WE WALK OVER THERE AND CONFRONT THE **ENEMY CHICKEN** AND THERE'S NO WAY Mrs Jingle Jangle AIN'T GONNA HEAR ABOUT IT. THOSE BIRDS CAN KICK UP ONE HELLUVA FUSS WHEN THEY WANT. IF SHE SEES YOU IT'S GAME OVER!

NO, I SAY WE GOTTA HIT 'EM WHEN THEY'RE
LEAST EXPECTIN' IT – WHEN THEY'RE UP
THAT TREE THINKIN' THEY'RE SAFE AS HOUSES.
CHICKENS GO TO SLEEP WHEN THE SUN GOES
DOWN AND THEY DON'T WAKE UP TILL IT
COMES BACK UP. I FIGURE THAT'S OUR WINDOW
OF OPPORTUNITY. I SAY WE GO BACK TO THE
WOODS AND PLAN."

I has no idea why he is talking about houses and windows, but **COW** seems to get it.

"ten four. woc copy that," she says, nodding in agreement.

Battle Planning

Hello.

I has been remembering how scared I was the last time I tried to get rid of the **EVIL CHICKENS**. There was two of us then: me and **Duck**. Now there is me, **Duck**, **COW** and **RUSTY**. This makes me feel a bit better. But I has to admit, not that much. When it comes to **EVIL CHICKENS** you just never know what's going to happen.

We sneaks back to our hidey-hole in the woods. **COW** is an incredible creeper. Even though she has had none of **RUSTY'S** special training, she seems to know exactly what she's doing.

RUSTY says we doesn't have time to expand our hidey-hole to make it big enough for her and all of us to fit in. **COW** soon shows him he needn't worry. Using her amazing **where's woc?** skills she hides in a nearby bush — all you can see, if you look really closely, are her big brown eyes. **RUSTY** is very impressed.

RUSTY renames our hole the War Room. **"FROM HERE WE DRAW UP OUR BATTLE PLAN,"** he says. **"SOLDIERS, LET'S HEAR YOUR IDEAS"**

"I reckon," Duck says, **"if *Fox* knew that the EVIL CHICKENS'** 'amazing' bribe was just an underfed turkey, I am sure he would change his mind about not eating them. If only we could get them out of the tree and over to his hole."

"I LIKE YOUR THINKING," says RUSTY. "NOTHING LIKE CRUSHING DISAPPOINTMENT TO SHARPEN THE APPETITE. BUT WE AIN'T GONNA BE ABLE TO GET THEM TO *Fox*, NOT WHILST THEY'RE ALL HOLED UP IN THAT TREE."

"Shame you can't fly like **Duck**, or climb like **COW** — if you could get up there you could chase them down," I says.

RUSTY slowly shakes his head. "SOLDIER, I MAY BE EXTRAORDINARY IN MANY WAYS, BUT HAVE YOU EVER SEEN A DOG CLIMB A TREE?"

"Hmmmmm," says **Duck**, thoughtfully stroking his beak. "**There has to be a way to get them all out. Has to be.**"

"**shakey! shakey!!**" says **COW'S** voice from inside the bracken bush. She gives the bush a big shake.

"**COW**," says **Duck**, "**this is no time for fun and games! We are doing serious planning over here.**"

I gets it. **COW'S** not being silly; **COW** is being smart.

"She's right!" I says. "While the **EVIL CHICKENS** sleep we shakes the tree so hard they falls out. They'll be dazed and half asleep; it'll make them easy for **RUSTY** to herd."

"**shakey, shakey, to fox, god takey!**" says **COW** proudly.

"**I LIKE YOUR THINKING, MA'AM,**" says **RUSTY**,

"BUT HAVE YOU SEEN THE SIZE OF THAT TREE? IT WOULD TAKE A WHOLE BATTALION TO MAKE IT SHAKE! THERE AIN'T ENOUGH OF US."

"How about the Sheeps?" I says. "Duck, remember how they itched themselves so hard on the Trocket it fell apart?"

"You know what, Pig, I think you're on to something," says Duck, looking rather surprised at my cleverness. "Those acorns must be doing wonders for your brain as well as your bottom!"

RUSTY doesn't look so impressed though.

"Sheep," he says, shaking his head and letting out a long sigh, "IT JUS' HAD TO COME DOWN TO Sheep, DIDN'T IT? DANG Sheep. THAT'S WHERE THIS OLD DOG'S JOURNEY BEGAN.

WITH THEM, AND THEIR CANTANKEROUS WAYS."

"What journey?" I asks. I realizes, apart from the soldier stuff, we knows so little about him. I can't imagine **RUSTY** having a problem with silly **Sheeps**.

"**WELL, I GUESS AS WE GOT A LITTLE TIME TO KILL RIGHT NOW...**" he says, leaning back against the wall of our hole. "**I MIGHT AS WELL GIVE YOU A DEBRIEF ON THE LIFE SO FAR OF RUSTINGTON-RUSTPATCH THE THIRD. SEE, I'M PEDIGREE JACK RUSSELL, BUT I WAS THE RUNT OF THE LITTER. SO INSTEAD OF GOING TO SOME FANCY-DAN HOME, I GOT SENT TO LIVE ON A Farm. GUESS NO PLACE ELSE WOULD HAVE ME. THEY ALREADY HAD TWO DOGS – SHEEPDOGS – AND THEY WEREN'T TOO FRIENDLY NEITHER.**

THEY LAUGHED AT ME. SAID
I WAS A SMALL WASTE
OF SPACE. SAID I'D
AMOUNT TO NOTHIN'.

SO I DECIDED TO SHOW 'EM. I DECIDED I'D LEARN
HOW TO HERD Sheep — SHOW 'EM I WAS WORTH
SOMETHIN'. BUT THE Sheep WOULDN'T PLAY BALL.
DAY AFTER DAY, COME RAIN OR SHINE, I WENT
OUT IN THAT FIELD. AND DAY AFTER DAY THEY
DISOBEYED ME; RAN RINGS AROUND ME. THE
SHEEPDOGS SAID I COULDN'T HERD A FLOCK OF
CHICKENS LET ALONE A FLOCK OF Sheep. THAT
CUT DEEP, BUT IT GOT ME THINKING: MAYBE IF
I PRACTISED ON SOMETHING SMALLER, LIKE
CHICKENS, I COULD HONE MY SKILLS; COME
BACK TO THE Sheep WHEN I WAS MORE PREPARED.

"I WAS YOUNG, I WAS FOOLHARDY, I WASN'T GOING TO LET ANYTHING STOP ME.

"SO ONE MORNING I GOT UP EARLY AND LET MYSELF INTO THE HENHOUSE. I THOUGHT IT'D BE A WALK IN THE PARK. I COULDN'T HAVE BEEN MORE WRONG. THOSE **CHICKENS** WERE BEYOND VICIOUS. THEY PECKED AND THEY STABBED AND THEY PECKED SOME MORE. I DON'T KNOW HOW, BUT I MADE IT OUT OF THERE ALIVE. BUT THAT DAY I LOST SOMETHING IMPORTANT TO ME..."

He glances down. I is sure he looks at his missing leg. Surely not!

"I LOST MY PRIDE," he continues, shaking his head. "I WAS A LAUGHING STOCK. I FELT I HAD NO CHOICE BUT TO LEAVE. SO THAT'S WHAT I DID. I DIDN'T EVEN SAY GOODBYE.

I JUS' HIT THE ROAD AND I'VE BEEN ON IT EVER
SINCE."

He lets out a long sigh.

"pooooooor god!"

says **COW'S** bush.

"NO NEED FOR
SYMPATHY MA'AM,"

POOOOR GOD!

he says, his voice

returning to its normal gruff soldier style.

"CAN'T MOVE FORWARD IF YOU'RE ALWAYS
LOOKIN' BACKWARD. WE NEED Sheep? WE GO
GET Sheep! Duck, YOU, PIG AND I'LL GO REACH
OUT TO 'EM. COW, YOU KEEP EYES ON THE
TREE. WE NEED A HEADCOUNT. DON'T WANT TO
MISS ANY WHEN THE TIME COMES."

"**roger that!**" she says.

Sheep Activation

Hello.

I has to be honest, I is never sure with **Sheeps** if they really is as silly as they seems, or whether they is just super stubborn. Whichever it is, dealing with them is tough. **Duck** says he is happy to do the talking. Their language is pretty simple. Even I understands most of it.

It's getting dark as we enters their field. They is all settling down for the night. But when they sees us they gets up. They spots me first.

"CAAARNIVAR! CAAARNIVAR!" they all chants as one.

Sheeps generally says everything together.
I sometimes wonder if they all has the same
brain, just in separate bodies.

Then they spots **RUSTY**.

"HAAAR! HAAAR!" they all laughs.

"SO SMAAAAALL!!"

RUSTY narrows his eyes and mutters
something under his breath what I can't
quite hear.

"NAAAAAR! PIG NO CAAAARNIVAR," says
Duck, shaking his head. "EVIL CHICKENS
FRAMED PIG FOR MURDAAAAAR. NOW THEY'RE

GOING TO DO SOMETHING NASTY TO OUR
TEMPORARY FARMAAAAAAR! NEED
YOUR HELP TO GET RID OF THEM FOREVAAAR."

The Sheeps all looks at Duck like he is
talking total nonsense; like he's not even
speaking their language.

"WHAAAAAT???" they all says, shaking their
heads and giving their cud a good chew.

"JUST LIKE I REMEMBER," mutters RUSTY.
"BUNCH OF IGNORAMUS WOOL BALLS!"

Duck takes a deep breath. "OK, I think
we need a new tack here. YOU LIKE BAAACK
SCRAAATCH?" he asks.

"OOOOH, YAAAAR! YAAAAR!" replies the Sheeps
enthusiastically, suddenly understanding
him perfectly.

"YOU COME TO OLD OAK TREE OVER THAAAAR TOMMORAAAAAR," he continues, pointing towards the woods. "WE HELP YOU GET BEST BAAACK SCRAATCH EVAAAR."

"OHHHH AAAAAR YAAAAR YAAAAR!" says the Sheeps. I can see from their eyes they has gone into a kind of trance just thinking about having a good scratch.

Duck does his best to make them understand that they needs to meet us at the tree just before sunrise. RUSTY says this is the best time — we needs a tiny bit of light so we can be sure we doesn't leave a single CHICKEN behind.

I really hopes they doesn't let us down.

We is only going to get one chance to stop the **EVIL CHICKENS'** terrible plan, and this is it!!

The Long Goodnight.

Hello.

I is writing this to you in the very middle
of the night. I can't sleep, I is too nervous.
If my handwriting is hard to read, it is
because it is very difficult to write in the
dark. I can hardly see my own trotter, let
alone what I is writing on.

When we got back from the **Sheeps**, it was
dark. The **EVIL CHICKENS** was already up
the tree and asleep.

COW reported back that there is eight
of them and that they all seemed very
"turnip" when they came back from the
Farm (if you doesn't know already,

"turnip" means "happy" in Pig. It's always
a happy time when you gets a turnip).
I knows exactly why they is happy too!
Because they has finished making their
horrible Pomb.

RUSTY says that all we can do now is play
"THE WAITING GAME". For a moment I thinks
that this is a real game and gets excited
– I loves playing! But it turns out he just
means we has to sit in our hole and wait
until morning. BORING!

"**I SUGGEST,**" he says, closing his eyes and
letting out a long breath, "**YOU TAKE THIS
TIME TO VISUALIZE THE BATTLE AHEAD. SEE
YOURSELF OVERCOMING THE ENEMY. PICTURE
THE SWEET VICTORY.**"

My problem is, whenever I thinks about the **EVIL CHICKENS** my tummy goes all churny and funny. Especially when I thinks about the SUPER EVIL one. I quickly decides to abandon **RUSTY'S** idea. I has a much better one: picture something that you likes and how you is going to enjoy eating it! Mmmmmm, slops, yummy, delicious slops I thinks, yum, yum, yum. This makes me feel much better.

But it makes my tummy feel very hungry. It lets out a loud rumble. **RUSTY'S** eyes fly open **"YOU GOT**

A MEGAPHONE IN THERE, SOLDIER?" he asks angrily, pointing at my tummy. "I MEAN WHY DOESN'T YOUR BELLY JUST SHOUT, 'HEY, CHICKENS, WE'RE HIDIN' OVER HERE!'?"

"Sorry," I mutters, feeling rather embarrassed. "I is just a bit hungry."

"BEST GET YOU SOMETHING TO QUIETEN THAT FOGHORN," he says, shuffling out of our hole and into the woods. A few minutes later he returns with an enormous pile of acorns. They is the most tasty ones I has eaten yet. Delicious.

Even though we is a little way from the tree, I can still hear the EVIL CHICKENS' snores. ZNORE! ZNORE! ZNORE! They is very loud.

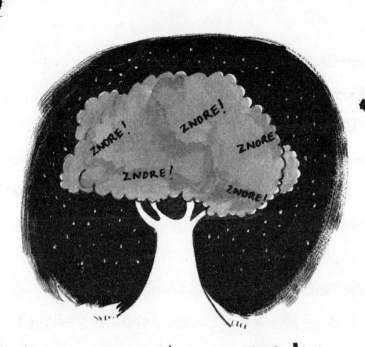

I hears a few rustles from **COW'S** bush
and a little yawn.

"Sleep tight, **COW**," I whispers.

"**yooooo toooooo,**" she moos back.

Through the dark wood, I can just make
out the light in Mrs Jingle Jangle's van. Poor
Mrs Jingle Jangle — she has no idea what

horrible ending the **EVIL CHICKENS** has in store for her.

RUSTY sleeps in a way that looks like he could spring into action at any moment. As usual he sleeps with one eye open — tonight it's watching the tree.

I closes both of mine and tries to nod off. But I can't.

I looks down at **Duck**, curled up next to me. His eyes is closed, but I is not convinced he is asleep either.

"**Duck**," I whispers, "is you awake?"

"**No, I'm fast asleep and so should you be. We've got a big day ahead,**" he whispers back.

"You can't talk and be asleep," I says.

"**I'm sleep talking,**" he replies grumpily.

"I can't sleep," I whispers, "I is too nervous. What if this all goes wrong and Mrs Jingle Jangle is blown away and **Ki-Ki** gets eaten by **Fox** and I gets taken away by Deathra and then I never sees you again!"

"**Shhhh, Pig,**" he says, curling up against me. He feels nice and warm, like a feathery hot-water bottle. "**We have to believe it will be OK – we have no other choice. Now: GO. TO. SLEEP!**"

Operation Evil Chicken Down

Hello.

What I would like to write here is this: I was wrong to worry and everything went perfectly to plan. But I can't. I is starting to realize that in my life nothing ever goes the way I wants it to. GRRRRRRR!!!!!!!

RUSTY woke us just before dawn. Normally it takes me a while to wake up. But not today. As soon as he gives me a little nudge I is up. It is still dark; the **EVIL CHICKENS** is still snoring.

I hears **COW'S** bush give a little rustle. "**woc banding stye,**" she whispers.

"She says she's standing by," I translates.

RUSTY starts to do something he calls **"PSYCHING HIMSELF UP"**. This involves beating his paws against his chest and repeating **"C'MON, SOLDIER!"** over and over. I may be a soldier now, but I is not going to do that. My trotters is too big and hard — I'd really hurt myself. Instead I sits and watches through the trees, hoping the **Sheeps** isn't going to let us down.

They doesn't. They arrives on time. I can tell they is ready for a really big scratch; they is all twitchy.

"RIGHT, YOU BUNCH OF OBSTINATE, WOOLY-WIGGED WIND-UPS..." I hears **RUSTY** mutter to himself as they approach, **"YOU AIN'T**

MESSIN' THIS OLD DOG AROUND TODAY! SOLDIER
Duck, PLEASE ARRANGE
THE sheep IN FORMATION
AROUND THE TREE
AND TELL THEM
TO AWAIT MY
INSTRUCTION."

I looks up at **Ki-Ki**. I can just make
him out, hanging limply in the darkness.
He must be so scared – **Ki-Ki** hates the
dark. I looks across at **COW'S** bush. Her
eyes stares back at us. They doesn't look
nervous at all – they looks kind of mad.

RUSTY marches over to our hidey hole. He
has a mad look in his eyes, just like **COW**.
"**RIGHT**," he says, "**THIS IS IT. READY TO DO**

THIS THING?" It feels like he is saying this more to himself than us.

We all agrees **RUSTY** should be the one to herd them — he's had practice. The only thing I has ever herded is slops into my mouth.

As **COW** can't fit in our hole, **Duck** and I hides with her in her bush.

RUSTY steps towards the **Sheeps** and raises a front leg. The **Sheeps** all gets themselves into their itching positions. He silently counts from three down to one, takes a very deep breath, then drops his paw.

All the **Sheeps** begin frantically itching. **RUSTY** looks relieved. Up and down the **Sheeps** rub themselves. They really goes for it. The tree rocks a little. But it's nowhere near enough to shake the **CHICKENS** out. **RUSTY** signals for them to itch harder. They does — the tree starts to move a bit more.

But it's still not enough.

I hears a confused **EVIL CHICKEN** cluck. Then a few more, but none of them falls.

The **Sheeps** go even faster. They are now moving so quickly they're just a woolly white blur. Come on, **EVIL CHICKENS**, fall, please fall. PLEASE!!

But not one does.

I hears **COW** let out a loud snort. I glances across at her, but she's not there any more. She's charging at the tree.

booomfff! She hits it head-on with all

her might. The tree does a big rock – it sways one way then the other.

Finally a sleepy **CHICKEN** flops to the floor. Then another, and another. I counts: three. Five more to go.

COW walks back and takes another run-up. **booooomf!** She hits the tree again. The **Sheeps** continue frantically itching. The tree does another big sway. I is surprised **COW** hasn't knocked herself out. It's like her head is made of stone.

I hears the **CHICKEN'S** sharp little claws scrabbling to hold on, but they can't. Four more tumbles out. They plops to the ground like feathery puffballs. Plumf! Plumf! Plumf! Plumf! They lies there, still half asleep, dazed by their fall. Seven down. They're all there but one: the **SUPER EVIL CHICKEN** is still missing.

I looks across at **Duck**; he nods. We both runs out of the bush and throws ourselves, along with **COW**, at the tree one last time.

I is not sure **Duck**'s weight does much, but mine does. Down through the branches crashes the **SUPER EVIL CHICKEN**. It's a long way from the top.

It lands right in front of me. For a

moment it looks like it might be dead. But then one of its evil eyes pops open.

"**YOU!**" it says. "**WHAT ARE YOU DOING HERE, YOU SILLY STINK BAG? YOU SHOULD HAVE BEEN DESTROYED, JUST LIKE WE PLANNED!**"

I looks across at **RUSTY**, expecting him to start rounding them up. Now would be a good time, before they realize what's happening. But he just stands there, still as a statue. His eyes fixed on the **SUPER EVIL** one. This must be one of his special soldier tactics.

"**AND LOOK, FELLOW CHICKENS**," continues the **SUPER EVIL** one, getting to its feet and letting out a cruel laugh. "**LOOK WHO THE BIG PORK SAUSAGE HAS BROUGHT WITH HIM FOR COMPANY.**"

All the **CHICKENS** scramble to their feet and turn to look at **RUSTY**. His tail drops between his legs and he starts to shake. This is the strangest way to herd I has ever seen, but I is sure **RUSTY** knows what he's doing.

"IF IT ISN'T THE LEGENDARY ICKLE PUPPY DOG, ONLY NOW HE'S BIGGER. WELL, SORT-OF BIGGER. KLA! KLA! KLA!" cackles the **SUPER EVIL CHICKEN**. "EVERY CHICKEN ACROSS THE LAND KNOWS YOUR PATHETIC TALE: GOOD NEWS TRAVELS FAST IN OUR COMMUNITY. COME TO SEE US SO WE CAN FINISH THE JOB OUR COMRADES STARTED ALL THOSE YEARS AGO, HAVE YOU?"

RUSTY'S back leg starts to twitch.

"Come on, **RUSTY!**" I whispers at him. "What is you waiting for?"

"YES, WHAT EXACTLY IS YOU WAITING FOR?" says the **SUPER EVIL CHICKEN**, doing a bad impression of me. "MEMORIES FLOODING BACK, ARE THEY? OH, HOW I HEARD YOU

HOWLED AND CRIED. YOU POOR LITTLE THING." It walks over and stands right in front of **RUSTY**. "**BOO-HOO, WAAAA-WAAAAA!**" it says, rubbing its eyes with its wings.

"I ... I..." stammers **RUSTY**. He no longer look like the soldier **RUSTY** we knows. He looks like a scared little puppy.

"**RUSTY!**" I cries out. "WE NEEDS TO GET THEM TO **FOX**. NOW!!!!"

"**WE DON'T HAVE ANY TIME FOR ANY OF THAT NONSENSE**," laughs the **SUPER EVIL CHICKEN**. "**WE'VE AN OLD LADY WHO NEEDS OUR SPECIAL ATTENTION, DON'T WE, COMRADES?**"

"**YA! YA! YA!**" nod all the **EVIL CHICKENS**, laughing.

COW lets out a huge burst of hot air from her nostrils.

"EEK! NOW MRS BEEFBURGER IS GETTING HER KNICKERS IN A TWIST TOO. WHAT ARE YOU GOING TO DO, DEAR? STEAM US TO DEATH WITH YOUR HOT BREATH?"

COW looks like she is about to explode with anger. The **Sheeps** all stops their itching and stares over. But **RUSTY** is still glued to the spot, trembling. Above me I hears **Ki-Ki** let out a weak little moan.

"YOU IS NOT GOING TO GET AWAY WITH THIS!!" I cries. "We is going to rescue **Ki-Ki**, prove that you set me up and stop you blowing up Mrs Jingle Jangle. Just you watch."

"**OH, REALLY?**" says the **SUPER EVIL CHICKEN** between sobs of laughter. "**YOU AND WHOSE PATHETIC ARMY?**"

"IF I HAS TO," I roars, moving forward and bearing my teeth, "I'LL DO **FOX'S** JOB MYSELF! I IS AN OMNIVORE, YOU KNOW!!" I is so angry that I feels like I might actually be able to do it (if I closes my eyes tightly and pretends they is feathery turnips). No one treats my friends like this.

All the **CHICKENS** suddenly shuts up and takes a step back. Ha! I thinks. Now who's laughing? I takes another step forward; the **CHICKENS** takes another one back.

"YEAH, WHO'S SCARED NOW?!" I booms in my biggest voice, feeling the most powerful I ever has.

"**I THINK YOU'LL FIND ... YOU ARE**," says the **SUPER EVIL CHICKEN**, pointing his wing over my shoulder. I turns my head to see what he is talking about.

My heart jumps so hard that it makes my body rock. There, crashing though the woods behind us, are Deathra. I can just make their white suits out through the greenery. I turns back to the **EVIL CHICKENS**, only they is no longer there. They're sprinting across the Sheeps' Field towards the **Farm**.

"**No time to lose!**" says Duck. "**COW, up the tree fast as you can!**"

"roger that!" says **COW**, pushing her way through the **Sheeps**. Quick as a flash she climbs up the trunk.

"NAAAAR WAAAAAY!!" baas all the **Sheeps**, standing back to watch in amazement.

Deathra crashes through the brambles and bushes, getting closer by the second.

COW frees **Ki-Ki** from the tree, and he flops to the floor in a heap. I rushes over and gently picks him up in my mouth. **"Moonstone doesn't feel too good..."** he manages to murmur weakly. He is still alive, but only just.

I hears a cry from behind us. I looks back. Big Deathra has fallen into our hidey-hole. He crawls out holding his ankle and screaming in pain.

His shouts snap **RUSTY** out of whatever weird trance he is in. He takes one look at them and turns to us.

"**I'M SO SORRY. I'M SO SORRY. I DON'T KNOW WHAT CAME OVER ME,**" he says, shaking his head. "**FOR A MOMENT THERE I WAS BACK IN THAT HENHOUSE AND... OH, HELL, NONE OF THAT MATTERS NOW. YOU MUST SAVE YOURSELVES. SAVE** Mrs Jingle Jangle. **I'LL TAKE CARE OF THEM. IT'S THE LEAST THIS OLD DOG CAN DO!**"

"No!" I tries to shout, but I can't get the word out with **Ki-Ki** in my mouth.

Little Deathra helps drag Big Deathra out of the hole.

"I LET YOU DOWN, SOLDIER PIG. LEAVE ME. THIS IS THE WAY IT MUST BE," says **RUSTY**.

"COME ON!" shouts **Duck**, tugging at my leg. **"He's right, we have no choice. We have to get out of here. NOW!!!!!!"**

I gives **RUSTY** a soldier salute. I feels it is the right thing to do. Then I turns and runs as fast as I can.

Behind me I hears Deathra's loud hisses. **RUSTY** starts barking, louder than I has ever heard him. His barks echo in my ears as I runs across the field. Brave, brave **RUSTY**, will I ever see him again?

The Last Hurrah!

Hello.

As I write this my heart is still pounding. I wonders if it will ever beat slowly again.

Duck, COW and me runs as fast as we can back to the yard. **Ki-Ki** flaps from side to side in my mouth. I wishes we has time to stop so I can check on him, but we doesn't. The **EVIL CHICKENS** is fast and they is determined. We is going to have to be even faster and more determined if we is going to stop them.

When we gets to the edge of the yard the sun has only just come up. There is no lights on in Mrs Jingle Jangle's van – she's still asleep.

I spies the **SUPER EVIL CHICKEN** and Number Two hurriedly rolling something large, brown and round towards the van. It has a long wire sticking out of the top of it.

"**the big pig bum!**" says **COW**.

She's right – they're planting the Pomb and they're not wasting any time.

I doesn't even stop to think. I plops **Ki-Ki** down and rushes straight towards them. I is much bigger than they is. I can stop them: knock them over, take the detonator — do something, anything to spoil their plan.

Just as they reaches the van they spots me and stops.

"Give me the Pomb, or else!" I hisses in my most fierce voice.

The **SUPER EVIL CHICKEN** narrows his eyes and stares straight at me. For a moment I actually thinks it might be taking me seriously. But then it gives me a nasty, evil little smile.

"**I DON'T THINK SO, STINK BAG!**" it says. "**COMRADE,**" it continues, turning to Number Two, "**THE TIME HAS COME TO GIVE**

YOURSELF IN THE NAME OF OUR CAUSE. ARE YOU READY?"

"INDEED I AM! NOTHING WOULD MAKE ME PROUDER," replies Number Two, puffing up its chest feathers.

"GOOD," nods the SUPER EVIL CHICKEN, "THEN PLEASE COMMENCE THE *GUARD THE BOMB AT ALL COSTS, ESPECIALLY FROM FATSO THE PIG* PLAN WITH IMMEDIATE EFFECT."

Number Two salutes and hops up on to the top of the Pomb. It starts twisting from side to side. As it does it begins to sink down. My poo is quite soft; soon most of Number Two has sunk inside. It pops its wings out and the SUPER EVIL CHICKEN hands it the detonator.

"**NOW, MR BACON SANDWICH,**" says the **SUPER EVIL CHICKEN,** poking me roughly in the chest with its wing, "**YOU SO MUCH AS BREATHE TOO CLOSE TO OUR BOMB AND NUMBER TWO WILL DETONATE IT, IMMEDIATELY!**

"**NUMBER TWO, PRIME THE BOMB AND START THE COUNTDOWN FROM SIXTY. THAT SHOULD GIVE ME PLENTY OF TIME TO GET INTO A SAFE POSITION TO WATCH THE SHOW,**" commands the **SUPER EVIL** one, giving the Pomb a hard kick. It and Number Two rolls under the van.

"**OH, AND NUMBER TWO...**" it calls out, "**COUNT IN PIG. I WANT OUR 'FRIEND' HERE TO BE ABLE TO SAVOUR EVERY LAST MOMENT. KLA! KLA! KLA!**"

"**YES, MASTER,**" clucks back Number Two from under the van, "**IT WOULD BE MY UTMOST PLEASURE! COMMENCING COUNTDOWN NOW: 60, 59...**"

The **SUPER EVIL CHICKEN** turns and runs back to my house, laughing.

60,59...

"**Quick, Pig! I've got an idea,**" says **Duck,** frantically beckoning me. I runs over. I REALLY hopes it's a good one — his best ever, in fact.

"**Now as I see it we only have one option left. We can't save the van but we can save** Mrs Jingle Jangle," he says, talking so fast he doesn't even stop to breathe. "**We have to get her out of there. Pig, I want you to take Ki-Ki and stand in the middle of the yard. COW, get over there and ring her doorbell. I'll keep an eye out for the EVIL CHICKENS; distract them if necessary. When she opens the door, Pig, you show her Ki-Ki. She should come running out to get him. COW, don't hang around. You get out of there as soon as**

Mrs Jingle Jangle **is out of that van. Got it?"**

"**oscar kilo!**" says **COW**. She gives us both a nod and runs over to the door. I takes **Ki-Ki** out into the middle of the yard and gently places him on the ground.

"**52, 51, 50...**" continues Number Two's voice from under the van.

COW lifts up her hoof and presses the bell. We waits. Nothing happens; no sign of Mrs Jingle Jangle.

"**bell no bing bong!**" she says, looking back at **Duck**, her voice echoing around the silent yard.

Number Two's counting speeds up.

"**47, 46, 45, 44...**" **Duck** frantically signals

to **COW** to bang on the door with her hoof. She bangs on it so hard her hoof almost goes straight through. It does the trick though. The door opens and a very confused-looking Mrs Jingle Jangle peers out. Her hair looks madder than ever. She rubs her eyes and pulls on her little round glasses.

"Look!" I whispers as loudly as I can (I doesn't want Number Two to hear and speed up even more). "Look, it's **Ki-Ki**! He's alive!!" I knows she won't understand a word what I is saying, but I wants to get her attention. I gently nudges **Ki-Ki** with my nose. He makes a weak little turkey noise.

Mrs Jingle Jangle looks at me, then down

at **Ki-Ki**. Her eyes bulge bigger than I has ever seen a **Farmer**'s eyes bulge. She holds her hands up to her face and lets out a terrible scream. It sounds like:

"AGHHHHHH! GOATS!!!!!"

She turns and slams the door and locks it. I doesn't understand what's going on. How could she confuse us with goats? She knows who we is!

"**33, 32, 31...**" continues Number Two, faster again.

Duck rushes over. **"Drat, she thinks you're ghosts. It must have been the whispering. We're running out of time,"** he says, looking panicked, **"and I'm running out of ideas. We're going to need some kind of miracle to save her now!"**

"god!" cries **COW** pointing over towards the Sheeps' field, **"god's coming!!"**

We both turns and looks at where she's pointing. In the distance I can just make out the **Sheeps** thundering across their field. And running round and round them, frantically barking orders, is **RUSTY**. He's alive!

"Look, it's **RUSTY**! He's finally controlling the **sheeps**," I shouts.

But then I spies two white lumps bouncing up and down on top of them. It's Dethra. They is being carried across the field, herded by **RUSTY**, right towards the yard. Little Deathra pokes at the **Sheeps** with his nasty electric stick. But rather than hurting them, it seems to be making them happy. Very happy.

"YAAAR! YAAAR! ELECTRIC BACK SCRATCHAAAAR!!" they baas as they runs towards the gate.

What is **RUSTY** doing??? He was supposed

to be keeping Deathra away. Not bringing them to me.

The **SUPER EVIL CHICKEN** struts out of my house to see what's going on.

"**HA! PIG, YOU NINCOMPOOP LOSER!**" it squawks at me. "**DOUBLE-CROSSED BY A THREE-LEGGED DOG. HOW VERY YOU.**"

"**27! 26! 25!**" shouts Number Two triumphantly.

The Sheeps reach the gate and crash through it. Deathra still bouncing wildly around on top of them.

"**DON'T WORRY, SOLDIERS. I'VE GOT IT ALL UNDER CONTROL!**" cries **RUSTY**, herding the Sheeps right at me. For a moment I thinks they is going to run me over. But just before they

does **RUSTY** barks an order to stop. Deathra
flies forward and lands right in front of me.

The **SUPER EVIL CHICKEN** was right.
RUSTY has brought Deathra to re-catch me.
I can't believe it. Why does I always trust
the wrong animals????

"**RUSTY**, HOW COULD YOU?" I cries.

Deathra picks themselves up and dusts

themselves down, angrily hissing as they does. I looks at **RUSTY** for some kind of answer. But he's not looking at me; he's looking up at the pointy arrow thing what **COW** hid behind the other day.

"**GOOD NEWS, SOLDIER PIG. WE'VE GOT A SOUTH-WESTERLY BREEZE; IT'S BLOWING STRAIGHT INTO YOUR HOUSE,**" he says, totally ignoring my anger.

"**21, 20, 19...**" continues Number Two excitedly.

Deathra hiss something at one another and step towards me.

"**REMEMBER, REVENGE IS A DISH BEST SERVED WARM AND STINKY. YOU KNOW WHAT YOU GOTTA DO, SOLDIER PIG,**" barks **RUSTY**. "**SNF!**"

"SNF?" laughs the **SUPER EVIL CHICKEN**. **"BET I KNOW WHAT THAT STANDS FOR: SEE NO FRIENDS!"**

"No," I smiles proudly. "No, that's not it at all. It stands for Silent ... Ninja ... Fart!"

As I says the words my bottom lets out the longest, most silent, ninja-ish fart I has ever done. My SNF is huge — it goes on and on. I feels sad when it finally finishes. It felt sooooo good. I catches a niff. It smells soooooo bad. Like no fart I has ever done before.

RUSTY was right about the wind direction; it blows my fart straight towards the **EVIL CHICKENS**. It hits the **SUPER EVIL CHICKEN** first. It starts to cough and choke. But

that's not all. Its head begins to swell and
foam starts to pour from its
beak. I hears the other **EVIL
CHICKENS** in my house start to
choke too. Soon the yard is filled
with the sound of **EVIL CHICKENS**
spluttering and wheezing.

The **SUPER EVIL CHICKEN**
collapses in a heap. Its eyes rolls round and
round. Its head is now twice its normal size.

"**GOOD WORK, SOLDIER PIG!**" cries **RUSTY.**
"**YOU'VE INFLICTED MORE DAMAGE THAN I EVEN THOUGHT POSSIBLE.**"

Both Deathra take a step back. They is no longer looking at me; they is looking down at the **CHICKENS**.

"CHICKENSHHHHH HASSSSSSSSHHHH DEASHHHHLY POXHHHHHH !!!!" hisses Big Deathra. "FETCHHHHHH SHEEEE VAN ISHHHHMMEDIATELY. WEEE MUSHHHHHH CATSHHHHHHH AND DESHHHHTROY SHHHHHEM!"

I looks to **Duck** to help me understand.
"**It's great; they can't smell your toxic fart through their helmets. They think the CHICKENS are contaminated with a Deadly**

Avian Pox!" he says. "**It's much worse than Swine Flu!!**"

Little Deathra runs off towards the road. The big one pushes me out of the way and flings open the door to my house. Inside the **EVIL CHICKENS** are all lying around twitching and drooling.

Big Deathra swiftly picks them up and tosses them into his net. The **SUPER EVIL CHICKEN** tries to say something. His voice is all high and funny. **"PIG, YOU..."** he

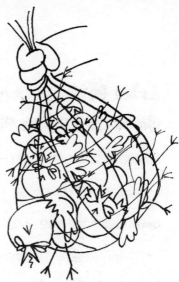

manages to squeak, but before he can finish, he's picked up by his neck and thrown into the net with the rest.

Deathra's white van screeches into the yard. The blue light on the top flashes. Little Deathra flings open the back doors. The big one throws the net full of **EVIL CHICKENS** in and then quickly slams it shut again.

"OMG!" I hears a weak voice croak, **"What's that seriously dee-sgusting smell?"**

It's **Ki-Ki**. My farts normally knocks him out, but luckily the wind didn't blow this one straight at him. A little niff of it has brought him around. UNBELIEVABLE! I looks across the yard. **Duck** helps him to his feet.

"Oh, **Ki-Ki**! Thank goodness you're OK!" I says, rushing over to him. "I thought I'd eaten you — and so did Mrs Jingle Jangle. But I hasn't. I is SO happy, and she will be too!"

"Eaten me? Really? You are soooo hilarious sometimes, Pig!" he says, falling into me and giving me a big feathery hug. I glances over my shoulder, expecting to see

Deathra coming to get me too. But instead
I sees their van screeching out of the yard.
They has forgotten all about me and **RUSTY**.
The **Sheeps** chases after them.

"**ELECTRIC BAAAACK SCRAAAATCHARRR!**" they
cries. "**COME BAAAAAACK!**"

I looks over at Mrs Jingle Jangle's van. The
door opens and she peers out. She MUST
have seen what happened, or at least heard.
How could she miss the loud siren and
Deathra's shouts? She can't possibly think
we is ghosts now. Deathra doesn't chase
ghosts!

"M ... M ... Moonstone?" she says.

"**Mrs Jingle Jangle!**" replies **Ki-Ki**,
letting go of me and turning to face her.

"Oh! Mrs Jingle Jangle, **I thought I'd never see you again!"**

Though she clearly has no idea what he is saying, I think she knows he's trying to speak to her.

"MOONSTONE! OH, MOONSTONE!" she cries with delight, running across the yard. She picks him up in her arms and hugs him tight. Then she sees me; in her excitement she must have forgotten she thinks I is an evil killer.

She stops being happy and takes a step back. Luckily, **Ki-Ki** understands what is happening straight away. He reaches down and starts to stroke the top of my head whilst making happy **Turkey** noises. I looks up and gives her my best, "I am a really nice, healthy Pig. Honestly!" smile.

She shakes her head, muttering to herself. For a moment I worries it's something bad, but then she reaches down and gives me a little stroke too.

"Sorry. So sorry," she says, giving me a gentle rub. I doesn't understand much **Farmer**. But I knows what this means.

It means that maybe, just maybe, everything is going to be OK.

She turns and carries **Ki-Ki** back over to her

van. She carefully puts him in the sink and gently starts to wash his dirty feathers.

For a moment everything seems perfect, but then I hears a loud squawk.

"12, 11, 10..."

It's Number Two. It's still under the van. It totally avoided my SNF, and, worse still, it's still stuck in the Pomb.

"**big pig bum about to go boooom!!!!**" cries **COW**.

Ki-Ki looks over at us from the sink and gives us a wave. He has no idea what is going on.

"GET OUT OF THERE! YOU'VE GOT TO GET OUT OF THERE!!!" I shouts at him. But just as I does, Mrs Jingle Jangle takes out this

strange, long, thin noisy thing
and starts drying him with it.
The sound of it drowns
out my cries.

"9, 8!!!" shouts
Number Two
merrily.

RUSTY sprints across
the yard and throws himself under the van.

He reappears, quick as a flash, rolling the
Pomb and Number Two out with his nose. He
pushes it across the yard and out into the

Sheeps' field.

"7, 6..." squawks Number Two angrily at him as he nudges it along.

"RUUUUUSTY! NOOOOOOOOO!!!!!!!!" I shouts. It can't end like this. He just helped save my life and now he's going to be blown up by a Pomb made out of my poo!

RUSTY sprints towards the Sheeps' Pond, the Pomb bouncing along in front of him. He reaches the edge of it and stops.

"5, 4, 3..." screams Number Two. RUSTY takes a few steps back.

"2!!!!" Number Two cries, going bright red in the face.

RUSTY sprints at the Pomb, and gives it one last, hard shove with his nose.

"WUUUUUNNNNNN!" cries Number Two as

they all fly though the air into the pond.

SPLOSHHHHH!!!! They disappears under the water.

For a brief moment there is total silence. Then:

A huge mountain of water erupts into the air. I has never seen anything like it. It's enormous. It rains back down and then everything falls silent.

We all stands and stares at the pond in shock. I can't believe what **RUSTY** has done. He's sacrificed himself to save **Ki-Ki** and Mrs Jingle Jangle.

"**NAAAAAAARRRRRR!!!!!**" baa all the **Sheeps**, who have returned from chasing Deathra down the road.

"**poor god!**" moos **COW** sadly.

My heart sinks. My amazing new friend is gone – just like that. I feels a tear roll down my cheek. I watches as it plops to the floor. More quickly follow, plop, plop, plop!

"**I can't believe it!**" says **Duck.**

"Neither can I," I says between sniffs.
"We'll never see him again."

"**No, I really can't believe it,**" says **Duck**,
pointing over at the **Sheeps'** Pond. "**Look!**"

I looks over. Something white is swimming

quickly across it. It reaches
the bank, pulls itself out and
gives itself a good shake.

"**HOOOOOOOO-**
HAAAAAAAAAAAA!!!!" it cries,
rearing up on to its one back leg.

235

"RUSTY," I shouts, quickly whipping away my tears so he won't see them. "YOU'RE ALIVE!!!" I wants to rush over and hug him, but I knows this is DEFINITELY not what he would want.

"SURE AM, SOLDIER PIG!" he shouts back triumphantly. "WHEN THIS OLD DOG GOES, IT WILL BE WITH MORE OF A BANG THAN THAT!"

I looks back at the van. A proud Mrs Jingle Jangle gives **Ki-Ki** one final blast with the noisy thing. She's turned him into a huge, feathery puff-ball.

She picks him up and they steps back out into the yard. I can't believe they has absolutely no idea what just happened.

"**What?**" says **Ki-Ki**, looking at our

shocked faces. **"It's my feathers right? I can't believe how totes amazing they look either!"**

Roger, Over and Out

Hello.

I is VERY, VERY, VERY HAPPY to report that Deathra has not come back. **Duck** is 100% sure Mrs Jingle Jangle will have called them and told them that I doesn't have swine flu. HUGE, HUGE PHEW!

I is also REALLY HAPPY to say that we has seen no sign of the **EVIL CHICKENS**. **RUSTY** has been keeping the Old Oak Tree under surveillance for the last two days and has reported back that he has observed NCA: Negative **CHICKEN** Activity. He says he is pretty sure Deathra will have "dealt" with them swiftly.

He also says that if there was a medal for OBF – Outstandingly Brilliant Farting – he would award it to me, immediately. I wishes there was. I would love to have a medal, especially one for farting.

I really wants him to stay and teach us more soldier things. Having him around is so much fun. But sadly he says he can't.

"THE **EVIL CHICKENS ARE DUST. YOUR BACON'S SAFE**," he says. "IT'S TIME FOR THIS OLD DOG TO MOVE ON. ADVENTURE CALLS. IT'S IN MY BLOOD TO ANSWER."

I promises him I will never forget what he has taught me. Though I really hopes I never has to bury my poo in a hole, or sleep in the cold, dark, noisy woods again.

This morning, after breakfast, we all walks him over to the main gate and says our goodbyes.

"**good luck, god!**" says **COW**.

"**YOU TAKE OF YOURSELF TOO, MA'AM,**" says **RUSTY**, giving a little bow.

Duck and I thanks him for all his help and **Ki-Ki** gives him a special "bandana" that he's made from a scrap of material he found in Mrs Jingle Jangle's van. **RUSTY** looks rather pleased with it. I has to say it suits him.

We watches him as he walks away. Just as he gets to the big bend in the road he turns back to us and salutes.

"STAY SAFE, SOLDIERS!" he barks. "AND IF YOU CAN'T STAY SAFE, STAY SHARP!" And with that he walks around the corner and is gone. **Duck** reaches out and gives **COW**,

Ki-Ki and me a little pat. I thinks he would put his wings around us, but there is no way they is long enough.

"**Well,**" he says, "**that was really was quite some adventure!**" We all nods in agreement.

I can tell Mrs Jingle Jangle is still a bit confused about what happened. I is not sure, even if we could tell her, she would ever believe us. She is being super nice to all of us – just like she was before. Her slops hasn't got any better though. But now I knows about acorns I doesn't mind. I pretends to eats everything she gives me, but when she's not looking I secretly sneaks around the back of my house and pours them away. Then I heads into the woods and eats as many acorns as I can find.

Mrs Jingle Jangle has insisted that **Ki-Ki** now sleeps in her van. I has to say I does miss my lovely feathery pillow, but I is also very happy for him.

Just as the sun is setting **Mr and Mrs Sandal's** holiday bus pulls up and drops them off. We all rushes over to see them. They looks great. They has gone very brown. I wonders if yoga involves having mud baths. It looks like it from the colour of their skin.

They gives Mrs Jingle Jangle a huge hug and us all big pats and strokes. Mrs Jingle Jangle is great, but I never wants the **Sandals** to leave us again, ever. I wishes

I could pat and stroke the **Sandals** back, to show them how happy I is to see them.

Before bedtime **Ki-Ki** comes over and asks for a meeting. He has never asked us for one before; he must have something very important to say.

"**OMG!**" he says, flapping his wings around excitedly. "**You really won't believe what the tea leaves just told** Mrs Jingle Jangle!"

"That I is going to get an extra big helping of **Mr and Mrs Sandal's** delicious slops for breakfast?" I says hopefully.

"**No! It's much more amazing than that!**"

I would stop him and tell him that there

really is pretty much nothing more amazing than extra slops, but he is talking so fast it's impossible.

"Her tea leaves told her that I am not just a replacement for her Moonstone, but that I AM HER MOONSTONE!!!!"

"But how can you be?" I asks. "You is a turkey; you looks nothing like a cat!"

"I know! I know!" babbles **Ki-Ki.** **"It's totally crazy. She looked into the leaves and started to cry with joy. Then she picked me up and started stroking me like a cat, saying,** "I knew it all along, Moonstone, it really is you. You've come back to me!" My **Farmer** is not great, but I got the gist. And honestly I think it's true. I've even started to feel like a cat. Listen to my purr: gobble-rrrrrrr, gobble-rrrrrrr."

"That's really, err, great," says **Duck**, giving me a wink.

"Well, it's sort of great, and then it's sort of not," says **Ki-Ki**, his excitement suddenly turning to sadness. His voice goes all wibbly-wobbly as he continues. **"You know how much I love you. I mean, really, you've totally been the best friends anyone could ask for. I honestly can't thank you enough."** A tear rolls down his cheek. **"And I ... I ... I ..."** he stammers, **"I want you to know this is the hardest thing I have ever had to say.**

**But, if you don't mind, I'm going to go
and live with** Mrs Jingle Jangle, **in her van.**"
He just manages to get his last few words
out before he breaks into big sobs.

"Please don't cry," I says, patting him
as gently as I can with my trotter. "This
is great news. We'll all miss you very
much, but knowing you is very happy
will make us all very, very happy." As I

says the words I almost starts to cry too. I takes some deep breaths and just manages not to.

"**ki-ki turnip. woc turnip**," says **COW**, giving him a little lick.

"**They're right**," says **Duck**. "**We only want what's best for you. I am sure** Mrs Jingle Jangle **will come back and visit the Farm again, and when she does you can come and tell us all about the adventures you've had and what life is like being a cat.**"

"A turkey-cat. A Tat!" I says. Everyone laughs.

"**Oh, you really are the best**," says **Ki-Ki**, wiping his eyes with his wing. "**The very, very best!**"

As I sits in my bed writing all this I feels happy and sad all at once. Happy that I am safe and that I has such brilliant friends; **Duck** and **COW** really is amazing amazing amazing. And even the grumpy **Sheeps** is kind of great in their own way. And happy that the **EVIL CHICKENS** is gone once and for all. But sad that **RUSTY** has gone and now **Ki-Ki** is going too. It's not a nice feeling when your friends leave you. I hope that it isn't too long until I sees them both again.

I wonders if anyone will ever believe any of what I has written on these pages. Right now, even I finds it hard to believe — it feels like a crazy dream. But then in the far distance I hears a howl.

"YIPPEE-KI-YAAAAAAAAY!!!!!!"

And I knows it was no dream. It really
was a great, big, fat, totally bonkers
adventure. The craziest ever!

Lots of love,

Pig, **Duck**, **COW** and all the **Sheeps**.

xxxx

Read Pig's first top-secret diary!

And don't miss Pig's other
super-amazing diaries!

Visit Pig's EXTRA-ORDINARY website diaryofpig.com to find out more about him, ask him questions, discover fun Piggy activities and much much more.